GENE RODDENBERRY'S

Andromeda™

THROUGH the LOOKING GLASS

GENE RODDENBERRY'S

Andromeda™

NOVELS FROM TOR BOOKS

DESTRUCTION OF ILLUSIONS
KEITH R. A. DeCANDIDO

THE BROKEN PLACES
ETHLIE ANN VARE WITH DANIEL MORRIS

WAYSTATION
STEVEN E. McDONALD

THROUGH THE LOOKING GLASS
JOSEPHA SHERMAN

THE ATTITUDE OF SILENCE*
JEFF MARIOTTE

*FORTHCOMING

VISIT THE *ANDROMEDA* WEB SITE
AT WWW.ANDROMEDATV.COM

GENE RODDENBERRY'S

Andromeda™

THROUGH the LOOKING GLASS

JOSEPHA SHERMAN

A TOM DOHERTY ASSOCIATES BOOK
NEW YORK

TOR®

This is a work of fiction. All the characters and events portrayed in this novel are either fictitious or are used fictitiously.

GENE RODDENBERRY'S ANDROMEDA™: THROUGH THE LOOKING GLASS

Edited by James Frenkel

A Tor Book
Published by Tom Doherty Associates, LLC
175 Fifth Avenue
New York, NY 10010

www.tor.com

Tor® is a registered trademark of Tom Doherty Associates, LLC.

ISBN 0-765-30486-4
EAN 978-0765-30486-5

First Edition: February 2005

Printed in the United States of America

0 9 8 7 6 5 4 3 2 1

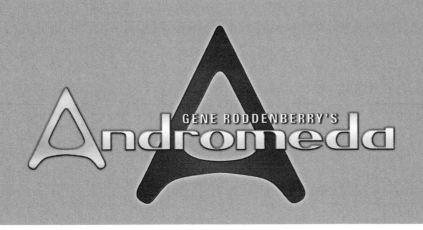

GENE RODDENBERRY'S

Andromeda

THROUGH the LOOKING GLASS

ONE · ANOMALY

Do not go gentle into that good night.

—DYLAN THOMAS

A better idea than that: Don't go there at all.

—DYLAN HUNT

It was, Captain Dylan Hunt thought, downright pleasant to, for once, be able to actually relax a little, settling back peacefully in his command chair. It was the first time in . . . however long it had been . . . that he'd had a chance to do this. A long time since he'd been able to acknowledge that, aside from it being a captain's command chair, with all the emotional impact that came with that status, the thing was actually rather comfortable.

All around the *Andromeda Ascendant* there was nothing but nothing, a nice, empty patch of space. It was the type of utter emptiness that was (assuming that your ship was in excellent working order and you had plenty of oxygen and other necessary supplies) downright peaceful in its lack of anything or anyone else. For a short time at least, Dylan thought with an inner smile, there was no one to fight, no one to attempt to befriend, no one to debate or otherwise try to persuade to join them or, for that matter, to leave them alone.

There was just open space, *Andromeda Ascendant*, and her small crew, who for once were not even arguing with each other.

Beka and Rommie—the latter there as a shimmering image "standing" next to Beka's console—were carrying on a quiet conversation that sounded as if it were about ancient and modern methods of navigation.

Seamus Harper, off with no one but a few bots in the Machine Shop, was happily working on a new, improved star analysis device with all the eager enthusiasm he always put into a new project.

Tyr Anasazi, completely alone and apparently liking that fact very much, was just as happily working out in Hydroponics, AKA (to him at least) the shipboard gym. For all Dylan knew, the Nietzschean was even trying once again to figure out what Dylan saw in that old Earth game, basketball.

Rev Bem was on the Observation Deck, lost in a tranquil Wayist series of meditations and, as far as the monk was concerned, not alone at all. He was at one, presumably, with the universe.

And Trance was doing, well, whatever it was that Trance was doing wherever it was she was doing it. No telling with her.

Just one big family, Dylan thought with a touch of wry humor. *That's us all right. One big, really weird, really dysfunctional family.*

Still, it wasn't a bad idea for everyone to have a few moments of downtime. Good for morale.

Including mine.

And of course the downtime couldn't last. Without any warning, Trance came rushing onto the Command Deck, her eyes wide and wild and their vision not quite focused, clearly seeing more than one level of existence or probability.

"Something's wrong!" she cried. "Almost wrong! Something is going to be wrong!"

Well, that was perfectly clear. For Trance.

"Could you be a little more specific?" Dylan began carefully.

But then Rommie broke in over his voice, starting up almost exactly at the instant that Trance finished. "Dylan, there's a good and immediate reason for her warning. My sensors are picking up something . . ." She paused, clearly making some swift analyses, then shook her head in an almost human fashion. "I don't know how to put this into words. I'll just say that we are about to get caught up in some truly strange disturbances in the space-time continuum."

So much for peace and quiet, Dylan thought.

All around the ship, what had been open space a moment ago suddenly exploded into a wild swirling of colors and patterns—red-violet, electric blue, green, gold, and colors that made no sense to human eyes, everything flashing, blazing and changing—fractals, spirals, eerie pinwheels of matter and glowing space dust. There should have been sound; the human brain wanted sound, maybe even some grand, cymbal-crashing music, to go with all that sudden chaos.

Beka summed it up for them all. Staring at the suddenly bizarre region of space erupting around them, she said, "What the hell is *that?*"

But without waiting for an answer from Rommie or anyone else, Beka sent *Andromeda* into a sharp banking turn to the left, so suddenly and with such force that Dylan just barely clamped his hands down on both arms of his chair in time, fighting to keep from being hurled right out of his seat.

"And what the hell was *that?*" he asked.

"Sorry. Didn't want to run us into . . . whatever that was."

"Anomalies." Rommie's voice was filled with static, and her formerly steady image rippled wildly in the air in front of Dylan, breaking up and reforming again and again.

There were times when Dylan forgot that Rommie wasn't human. And times when he was starkly reminded that she wasn't. Like right now. "What *kind* of anomalies?" he prodded.

"They . . ." There was the pause that meant Rommie was going through all her computer data. "There are numerous wormholes and . . . other, more unknown phenomena." Through the static, she managed to sound, well, almost embarrassed at having to admit that she didn't know what they were. "Some of the wormholes are merely pinholes, but others could swallow us if we make a mistake. And none of them are stable."

" 'We' meaning 'me,' " Beka said under her breath, just loudly enough for Dylan to hear.

Rommie ignored her, smoothly continuing, "What's more, there is no predictable pattern to their appearance or size."

"Yeah, right," Beka muttered. "I know the drill: Activate Live Pinball in a Pinball Machine Maneuver."

That was, a stray wisp of memory told Dylan, an archaic game from old Earth, one that was still found in some spaceport bars—which was presumably where Beka had learned about it. An archaic game, maybe, but he got the point.

"Hang on, everyone!" Dylan broadcast.

Over the next few minutes, Dylan silently agreed that, yes, being a Live Pinball in a really warped Pinball Machine really was what it felt like, with *Andromeda* twisting and diving and all but tying herself into knots without warning. Hanging on for dear life like everyone else, Dylan found himself suddenly wondering what would happen if only *part* of the ship, say maybe one of *Andromeda*'s engines, slipped into one of those constantly opening and shutting wormholes.

Not physically possible. I hope.

"Ships," Beka said suddenly, her voice tense with concentration. "Off starboard. A fleet of them."

"Rommie, report," Dylan ordered.

"They are unfamiliar ships," Rommie added after a pause as she put their images on-screen. "I have nothing on them in any of my databanks." She sounded a bit embarrassed about that, too.

Dylan frowned. "Beka?"

She spared them a quick glance, and then returned to her grim-faced "pinball" piloting. "New to me."

"Anyone?"

Trance shook her head. "No's" came in from Rev Bem, Tyr, and Harper.

The ships didn't look like any that Dylan had ever seen, either. Of course, that in itself wasn't very alarming, or even very surprising. Space was, to put it mildly, big, and there were many space-faring races out there, more than even Rommie could have cataloged.

She could, however, do a lot with what was available. After a few seconds, Rommie began efficiently rattling off statistics for the other ships, almost as though trying to make up for her previous lack of hard data: relative speed, relative size, relative weaponry.

She, Dylan thought, staring at the images on the view screen, could have added "relative beauty or lack thereof" to her categories.

Granted, starships didn't have to be streamlined, not as long as they stayed safely out in the frictionless vacuum of space and didn't enter any planetary atmospheres. But even allowing for that fact, the six vessels making up the approaching fleet could only be called one thing: downright ugly. They were as graceless and bulky as cargo freighters—but their engines looked alarmingly powerful, far more than any normal freighter would need. And those were definitely gun ports on their dull gray hulls.

Dylan frowned. "There's no reason to think them hostile, not yet. They're probably just caught up in the same rough patch of space—"

"They're powering up weapons," came from Tyr, who had practically dived for the weaponry console.

"—and then again," Dylan continued, "maybe not." How they hoped to hit anything, let alone a ship moving as swiftly and unpredictably as *Andromeda* in all this chaos . . . "Hold your fire, Tyr."

"But—"

"Hold your fire! You're not going to be able to hit them any more than—" He broke off abruptly as a blast of red fire shot from one enemy ship . . . and missed them by so wide a margin that it looked like a distant comet.

"Any more than they can hit us," Dylan finished levelly. "Get my point? Rev, you there?"

"I am," came the calm answer over the comm.

"See if you can open up any sort of communications with them. Find out who they are. And why," he added as another blast was fired off . . . and once again missed them completely, "they seem to hate us so much."

Meanwhile Beka was continuing her fierce swoops and turns of *Andromeda* without a second's hesitation, her lips back from her clenched teeth in a silent, determined snarl. At least, Dylan thought, they didn't have to worry about her being distracted from her work, even by unknown enemies with lousy aim. She was a pilot first and foremost.

"Sorry, Captain," Rev Bem said suddenly. "Nothing. Whoever they are, they most definitely don't want to talk with us."

"Why am I not surprised?" Dylan retorted. "Keep trying."

"I'm firing back at them!" Tyr snapped.

"No, you are not!" Dylan ordered. "Tyr, be sensible!" Assuming, of course, that a Nietzschean warrior with his blood up *could* be sensible. "Even you couldn't hit a target under these circumstances. And no, damn it, that wasn't a challenge! Don't waste ammunition, got it?"

There was a mutter of something hot-tempered from Tyr that Dylan prudently refused to hear. But at least Tyr seemed to have gotten the point of what Dylan was saying because he didn't fire.

"Good," Dylan said, "but now let's see about—"

Beka's frantic yell cut across his voice. "Look out! Everyone—*look out!*"

Rommie's image winked out. *Andromeda Ascendant* slewed roughly sideways in space, for the moment utterly graceless, and Dylan—

—was suddenly enveloped in dazzling blue-white light, unable to see, barely able to hear—

We've been hit! he thought wildly. *One of the anomalies, whatever it is, whatever it's doing to* Andromeda—

"Dylan!"

That was Beka's shout. He dimly heard the others shouting in alarm as well, something about him, something about, "Dylan's gone!"

That didn't make sense. He was right here—wasn't he? Everything was surely normal, if chaotic, light had never hurt anyone, no matter how garish, and *Andromeda Ascendant* and her crew were real and solid about him—

No!

In the next second, there was nothing, there was nowhere, there was no up or down, there was no sight, sound, scent, no solidity, there was barely a feeling even of self, just one flash of utter terror of this all at once *not being* and room for only one quick thought:

Is this death?

No one answered.

But now there seemed to suddenly *be* a "now" again. Without any sense of how much time had passed, if it had at all, he was solid once more, in that instant knowing that he was once more Dylan Hunt. He also knew, without knowing how he did, that what had been his reality had just dissolved itself and re-formed itself about him in quite a different way.

Re-formed itself into, uh, what?

As his brain and vision cleared, Dylan straightened, standing frozen in sheer, disbelieving shock. About to yell to Beka, *Get Rev Bem in here, fast, I think I'm finally going out of my mind*, he closed his mouth again. Oh no, all this was just too tangible in every sharp detail to be nothing but some strange, anomaly-born delusion.

All right, panic wasn't going to help him. And it wasn't as though absolutely everything was wrong. This was still the *Andromeda Ascendant*.

Or maybe that should be, this was *an Andromeda*. It certainly wasn't *his Andromeda*. There was the same general shape to the Command Deck, but apparently Rommie, if Rommie this still was, had suddenly and arbitrarily decided on a completely different color scheme. It was a truly ugly one, too, with walls and consoles now painted in a narrow spectrum of dull greens and browns that were spiced up with an occasional misplaced jolt of garish orange.

Someone has a really terrible sense of design.

And while he was on the subject—the current crew wasn't exactly a thing of beauty, either.

But then, the *Andromeda* he knew was not and never had been crewed by man-sized biped green-scaled dinosaurs.

"Toto," Dylan said, "I don't think we're in Kansas anymore."

TWO • THE *ANDROMEDAE*

For every action, there is an equal and opposite
reaction.

—SIR ISAAC NEWTON,
THIRD LAW OF PHYSICS

For one truly bizarre moment, Dylan was sure that it was his
crew who had been miraculously turned into . . . dinosaurs?
But that didn't make any sense at all.

Of course, neither did this.

Fortunately, the dinosaurs, the saurians, whatever they
were, were just as stunned by Dylan's sudden materialization as
he was. He really doubted that he could have handled a rush by
all five.

They were bipeds, and roughly of human height and shape,
but definitely more powerfully built. Their hands bore long,
curving claws, and their heads were . . . well, Dylan decided

quickly, their ancestors must have had elongated lizard jaws—
velociraptors, his mind whispered. Evolution had rounded their
species' faces, but they were still made up mostly of jaw, one
smooth arc of bone from forehead to what would have been
chins in human faces.

Their slit-pupiled eyes glared at him, glinting orange, and
their bodies were covered with those dull green scales. Possibly because of the natural covering those scales provided, they
wore only trousers of some dark, smooth material—and hol-
sters holding impressive-looking side arms.

Intelligent dinosaurs. Well, that wasn't impossible. He'd
heard or maybe read somewhere that back on old Earth, scien-
tists had found velociraptor fossil skulls with indications that
that particular species of dinosaur had been developing more
complex brains than the other dinosaurs. If that infamous meteor hadn't hit and if mammals hadn't managed to advance
into the top evolutionary slot, velociraptors might have been
the ones to fill the intelligence niche instead.

No meteor strikes on their *world, I'd guess. No mammals, either.*
Or else these guys' ancestors ate them all.

And how in hell did I get here—wherever "here" is?

Part of his mind, which was trying relentlessly to be logical
in the face of all this madness, went right on analyzing the
saurians. They were presumably not as warmblooded as humans, since the ship's temperature was warm verging on hot,
although it wasn't unbearably hot, fortunately for him.

Like humans, the saurians varied slightly in height and
weight, as well as in skin color. Some of them were a darker

green than others, or rougher of scales. But, a little unnervingly, the saurians gave him no clues whatsoever as to which of them were male or female—assuming that their species even *had* male and female.

Look, I don't care if they reproduce by budding. I just want to know where I am and why I'm here!

But before he could organize his stunned brain to say anything, a dark-green saurian exclaimed, "Look at him! Those are not scalesss covering his body—they are full-covering clothesss! He isss v'hun of the smooth-skinsss!"

The ferocity with which those words were spat out gave Dylan an alarming glimpse of sharp fangs.

Carnivore fangs.

Of course. I couldn't get thrown in among herbivores, oh no. That would be too simple. This just keeps getting better and better.

"V'hait," another saurian said, his voice—*maybe* it was a male—chill and utterly without emotion. "That isss not a sensible conclusion. Neither the smooth-skinsss nor v'he have the technology for a transfer such asss v'he have just, undeniably, v'hitnessed. Nor do the smooth-skinsss hide their naked skinsss in such a strange fashion. Their coveringsss are more primitive, not like v'hat thisss one v'hears at all.

"You, who are you? V'here isss Captain Huun't?"

I understand them, Dylan realized with a new shock. *I shouldn't be able to understand them.*

Whoa, wait, unless . . .

Oh. Oh no, that can't be.

Yes, but that would explain a lot.

Hey, there are *alternate dimensions,* he argued with himself. *At least in theory. And this is no stranger than being three hundred years out of my birth time.*

Oh yes it is! himself argued back at him.

"*I* am Captain Hunt," Dylan told them, testing his sudden theory and enunciating very carefully. "I am Captain Dylan Hunt of the *Andromeda Ascendant.*"

"That isss a foolish claim," the logical one said without heat. "*Androom'da* isss *thisss* ship called."

"And Captain Huun't isss not so hideously smooth-skinned!" cut in the dark green saurian.

Oh joy, Dylan thought. *I'm right. I really have been tossed into another dimension. Just me, apparently. Through some personal wormhole or, ah, some private beam of light.*

Well, I suppose a personal transport beam is better than finding out that I really did go insane back there.

"Look, never mind my, uh, hideous smooth skin," Dylan said to them all. "Just tell me this much: Did your ship just go through some bizarre spatial anomaly? Just before the switch happened?"

"V'he do not talk v'hith the smooth-skinned kind!" the dark green saurian insisted angrily.

I just bet *you're the Tyr analogue in this place,* Dylan thought. *Just as arrogant and just as hot-tempered.*

Well, if this was Tyr, then that slim saurian by the far console might be female, a scaly version of Beka. He could use that.

"Name calling isn't going to get us out of this predicament,"

Dylan said, trying to keep his voice as coldly controlled as that of the first saurian. "Neither, I'll add, is prejudice."

The logical one retorted indignantly, "V'he do not fall subject to such v'heaknessesss."

"Of . . . course you don't. That was just a pet name you all have for my species. All right, never mind that," Dylan added quickly, seeing them all rousing. "Look, I'll prove something to you: I know your names. One of you is called Beka."

To his surprise, the slim saurian that he'd mentally selected as Beka's analog never moved. Instead, the most burly, least feminine looking of the five took a half step forward. "I am Bekha." The voice was a definite baritone. "How do you know thisss fact?"

Beka the Fullback, Dylan's mind gibbered. *When I get back, I'll have to tell her that her counterpart could try out for the New Zandi Victors and make the team look like wimps—*

If I get back, that is—

He grimly broke off that thought. If there was a way here, there had to be a way back as well. He would not accept that this had been a one-way trip. "And one of you is called some variation of 'Harper,' right?"

That, judging from the start that particular saurian gave, was the identity of the logical one.

Okay . . . if you say so. Harper can be called many things, and certainly has, but "logical" isn't one of them.

"And there's a variation of 'Trance'?" Dylan continued hastily. "Yes? And there's a Rev Bem, isn't there?"

He'd been right about the argumentative dark green saurian

being the Tyr-analogue; his name here was Tyr'h. The Trance aboard this ship turned out to be the slim saurian, Tra'ansss. The Rev-analogue was called Bh'em. Bh'em gave Dylan a moment of genuine shock, since the Rev on this version of *Andromeda* was—unlike the Rev he knew so well—almost beautiful, as sleek as a greyhound, with smooth scales that were a lovely pale Nile green. Most startling of all was the realization that this Bh'em was not of an alien species to these folks, the way that Rev Bem was to the humans on *Andromeda*. No, he was clearly just a variant of the same species.

All right, I get the point. I can't take the parallels between my ship and this one too far.

"I thought so!" Dylan forced himself gamely onward. "You did go through an anomaly zone, just as my crew and ship did. And your Captain Huun't"—he did the best he could with that glottal stop and click—"your captain vanished at precisely the same time that I did. Yes, and since we all know that Nature abhors a vacuum, the old girl probably grabbed for the nearest equivalent of him, which was me, and of me, which was him, and dropped me here in his place. Yes, and that in turn means, since Nature does abhor that vacuum, that your captain is probably in my dimension, in my place on my ship right now."

Dead silence greeted that analysis.

Trying again, Dylan summarized, "We got switched. We're both captains of two different versions of the same ship in two different dimensions."

Still silence.

Then Bh'em, the Rev-analogue, said suddenly, "Korth'sss Fourth Theory isss true, it v'hould appear."

"Explain," the Harper-analogue returned.

"It isss quite obvious. For did Korth'sss and Suuranai not state in their second postulate on the theoretical sciencesss, *A Possibility of the Impossible*, that in the microverse of subatomic particlesss there are many possibilitiesss? That each of those particlesss isss either changed by observation, or that each particle in turn createsss a new universsse asss it splitsss off? So it isss also quite obviousss, then, assuming that v'he agree to the second postulate, that there may truly be many universsssess other than thisss, and that unexpected transitionsss may, indeed, occur."

"That's right," Dylan agreed helplessly. *Theoretical physics was never my strong point.* "Like it or not, I'm here, and as I say, your captain is probably on my ship in my place."

I'm not even going to try to keep up with the quantum whatevers that are involved.

Improvising wildly, Dylan added, "Clearly, the switch of the two of us means that there really is some sort of cosmic balance involved. And that means that if you want *your* Huun't back again, you're going to have to keep that balance steady and keep *this* Hunt alive. Otherwise there can't be a second switch that gets me home and brings back your captain.

"Besides," he added wryly as alarms suddenly sounded and the ship shook wildly, "this really isn't the time to argue about it. Your ship needs a captain, and she needs him right now."

Tyr'h, the Tyr-analogue, snarled at him, "Not one who isss a smooth-skinned freak!"

"You're good at name-calling, aren't you?" Dylan snarled back at him in his best Tyr Anasazi style. "It's so much easier than facing facts, isn't it? Enough of this for now! We'll settle it later."

"A promise."

Just then, the ship lurched again, so violently that Dylan and the saurians almost lost their footing. As Dylan grabbed for the nearest railing to keep from falling, he heard a female voice. It sounded almost alarmingly like that of his ship's Rommie—save for those saurian sibilants, and that utter coldness of tone.

"Argue at some later time. *Someone* must take command. I v'hill not be able to get usss through all these anomaliesss on my own."

Thank you, Rommie Two, or whatever you are.

"You heard that!" Dylan snapped, still imitating Tyr Anasazi with all his will. "This ship is in immediate danger. Navigation, Communications, all of you, get back to your posts. *Now!*"

By God, the act actually worked. As the crew got to work, Dylan heard Bh'em say in the emotionless voice that seemed more typical for these folks than Tyr'h's hot words, "If he isss, indeed, a parallel of the captain, then the logic of the situation meansss that he must know thisss ship as well."

Good.

But before Dylan could feel too smug about his success, he heard Bekha add, very softly, just loudly enough for him to hear it, "Inferior being though he isss."

Damn it. They just couldn't let the subject drop, could they? These guys were as stubborn and as arrogant—yes, and as prejudiced—as so many Nietzscheans confronting a mere "mongrel" of a human.

Right. And one of these stubborn, arrogant, downright prejudiced saurians is on my ship right now. In my place.

Lord. And how, I wonder, is my crew dealing with their new captain?

And am I ever going to find out?

THREE • THE OTHER

Cast your eye upon the Changeling,
then look for the origin of Change.
Perhaps it is in the Eye.

—LUNA,

"CATALOG OF COMPANIONS," CY 302

"Dylan!" Beka shouted in horror as the blaze of light and the eerie blurring engulfed him. "Dylan, get down, move, do something—

"God, no, he's gone!"

What followed was a brief time of utter confusion and wild shouts from them all of:

"Who—"

"Where—"

"Watch out!"

"What's happening?"

"Warning." That was Rommie's voice, inhumanly calm in

the face of all the confusion. "Captain Dylan Hunt is not aboard."

"Not aboard!" Beka all but snarled. "How could he not be aboard? Where could he have gone?"

Then, just as suddenly, the blazing light and the blurring was gone. The ship snapped back into clear definition, and . . .

"Dylan Hunt has returned," Rommie said, but now her voice sounded oddly . . . puzzled.

Not surprisingly. The figure who was standing now where Dylan had been standing just a moment ago . . . wasn't Dylan.

It wasn't even human.

Beka had her weapon drawn without even realizing that she'd moved. And Tyr, being a true Nietzschean warrior, must have started moving the minute he heard the first hint of commotion. He appeared on the Command Deck so suddenly he seemed to have appeared out of nowhere, already on full Nietzschean "take no prisoners" alert and ready to strike.

"We have lost the attacking ships," Rommie commented almost conversationally. "Our visitor could not possibly have come from one of them. There aren't any other vessels in the general region."

Then where did he . . . ? "All right," Beka said to the stranger. "Slowly, now. Who—and what—are you?"

The . . . being, whoever, whatever it was, looked as if someone had somehow crossed a human with a large, biped lizard. No, Beka thought, make that, rather, a strange cross with a muscular dinosaur, one who came complete with a covering of sleek green scales.

A civilized dinosaur, too, at least judging from the fact that it wore dark trousers, and had a holster at its hip. Oh, and now that Beka got a good look at its, uh, face, a definite, angry intelligence glinted in those alien, orange, slit-pupiled eyes. The saurian also was, Beka noted uneasily, almost exactly the same height as Dylan. A little too much of a coincidence, that last fact.

"I do not answer questionsss from smooth-skinsss!" it—no, he, that voice definitely sounded male—he retorted sharply. "Who and v'hat are *you*? V'here am I, and v'here iss my crew?"

Smooth-skins?

"Good questions," Beka agreed, putting on her toughest face, the one that said, mess with me and die. "But as the home team, we make the rules, and I rule that we go first. What happened to Dylan Hunt? And if you didn't expect to wind up here, how come we can understand you?"

The being stiffened as if she'd offered him a mortal challenge. "V'hat stupidity isss thisss? You understand me because v'he happen to be speaking the same language! That isss a fact that should be obviousss even to a smooth-skinned creature like you! Ask rather how it isss that *you* come to speak *my* language. And v'hat insanity isss that you babble about 'Dylan Hunt?' That isss not how it isss properly pronounced! I know this, because *I* am Dylan Huun't!"

"Like hell you are!"

"I do not lie!" The saurian glanced quickly around, his head moving not with the smoothness of a mammal but with the sharp, sudden moves of a reptile. "V'hat isss thisss place?"

"The Command Deck."

"Yesss . . . the shape of it isss right, the placement of consolesss isss right—but nothing else isss right! The colorsss of everything are ugly, everything clashing, everything too bright. And you, all of you are *wrong*, smooth-skinned beingsss, not my crew!"

"Smooth-skinned" again, eh?

"Rev," Beka murmured, "get up here, fast."

"On my way."

Trance, meanwhile, had silently moved forward, staring up at the stranger with her strange, intense, unblinking fascination. "He is *a* Dylan, all right," she said suddenly. "He's just not *our* Dylan."

Tyr snarled. "This is no place for mysticism."

"It's not mysticism," Trance returned without heat, and without turning away from the alien. He stared right back at her with what Beka thought was reluctant fascination: Trance often had that effect on people.

"He's a different Dylan, all right," Trance said after a second. "But definitely *a* Dylan, as I said. I think that all it is, is that they've just switched places."

"All?" Beka exclaimed.

The saurian recoiled. "Sv'hitched? Between my people and you smooth-skinsss? Between my ship and thisss abomination?"

"I *beg* your pardon!" Rommie exclaimed in what sounded very much like human indignation.

"How did thisss happen?" Huun't continued fiercely. "My

crew and I made no sv'hitch! V'he v'hould not! I v'hould not leave my ship! V'hat did you smooth-skinsss do to me?"

"We did nothing!" Tyr shouted back at him. "What did *your* people do? Where is Dylan Hunt?"

"Do you accuse *me* of thisss nonsense?" the saurian snapped back at him, fangs glinting. "V'hat isss this? Do you issue challenge?"

"He does not!" Beka snapped, moving between them and giving Tyr a warning glare. "We aren't accusing you of anything. Yet."

Huun't hissed at her. "I am a captain, assigned and honored as such. I v'hould not abandon my ship, my command!"

The indignation, Beka thought, sounded real. Just the way *their* Dylan might sound under the circumstances. Whatever they were. Wherever he was. Saurian or human, it seemed, captains were captains.

"All right, everyone, calm down." Beka glanced at Tyr again, who this time deliberately refused to meet her gaze. "Now, as our guest asks: Does anyone have any idea—any *plausible* idea—how this happened?"

Rommie's image shimmered back into existence. The saurian started and hissed with surprise. "You are not flesh-and-blood."

"You are observant." Rommie managed to put a world of sarcasm into the three words without showing as much as a hint of a smile.

"What, isss *thisss* your ship'sss persona?" Huun't asked the others.

"I am *Andromeda Ascendant*," Rommie agreed.

"But . . . *my* ship isss *Androom'da!*"

Rommie nodded. "That is quite possible."

"How so?"

"It would seem that the anomaly opened a temporary rift between two of the many possible universes," Rommie explained, "and that there was, indeed, an exchange. Why only these two captains were exchanged and not all of us, including me and my apparently other dimensional sister ship, is as yet unknown."

"Well, can we get our Dylan back?" Beka asked.

Rommie was silent for a disconcertingly long while. At last she said only, "Unknown."

"Are you saying that we've lost him?" Beka's voice sounded shriller to her than she'd intended. "That Dylan's stuck somewhere else and we're stuck here with this—this *lizard*?"

Huun't retorted just as sharply, "I am not a lizard—and I v'hill not be trapped here among thessse smooth-skinsss!"

Fighting down an angry shout since she'd already issued that warning to everyone else to stay calm, Beka forced herself instead to simply shrug. "You want to leave?" she asked. "Go ahead. We're in the middle of deep space, near a series of perilous and unpredictable spatial anomalies and there's not another ship around for who knows how many light years, but fine, feel free to go."

"I said unknown," Rommie cut in. "I did not say impossible."

"Well?" Beka prodded.

"I am already doing analyses of what data there is."

"Yeah, me, too," came Harper's voice over the open link to the machine shop in which he was currently working. "Rommie and I, we are hunting for the parameters of the rift."

The saurian hissed again, and this time it was a sound of sheer frustration. "Now I believe it. Thisss isss real. You have a Rhom'hai that isss smooth-skinned but just asss finely efficient asss our own."

"My efficiency remains to be seen," Rommie countered.

"That," Huun't countered, "v'hasss sarcasssm on my part."

"Hah," said Beka.

Just then, Rev Bem reached the Command Deck—and stopped short in astonishment, staring at the saurian.

"Hello, Rev," Beka said with fake cheerfulness. "Say hello to another Dylan Hunt of another *Andromeda*."

"*Thisss* . . . is Bh'em?" the saurian asked weakly.

"Ah," Bem said, recovering quickly. "I . . . ah. I see. The Force of Creation really does have a strange sense of humor, does It not?"

That, Beka thought, just about summed it all up.

"You," Huun't all but spluttered, "you. You are not one of the smooth-skinsss, yet you are not properly ssscaled, either. V'hat are you?"

"That is a difficult question, especially if one is to answer it simply," Bem said thoughtfully. "For eons philosophers have questioned who and what we all are without coming to any clear resolution." Only someone who knew him well could have caught the trace of humor in his voice. "Among the other roles that I am currently undertaking, I am a monk, a follower of the Wayist path, a Magog, and a member of the crew of *Andromeda Ascendant*."

He paused, blinking innocently. "Does that help you?"

"But you . . . thisss ship . . ." Huun't stopped and shook his head in what seemed a very human gesture of confusion.

But then he drew himself up proudly. "I accept v'hat I must accept. This isss indeed another dimension. I am here, and your captain mussst be in my dimension in my proper place. At least that much isss clear. This ship isss akin to my own, and so I shall be itsss steward, itsss captain, until I may return to my own command."

"We can't ask for anything more," Beka agreed. "Welcome aboard, Captain Huun't."

FOUR • OH CAPTAINS, MY CAPTAINS

Courage is the price that Life exacts for giving peace.
Which is probably why there's so little peace in the
universe.

—ARDAN LEFTAR, DIPLOMAT, RETIRED,
SPEECHES AND DISPOSITIONS, VOLUME THREE, CY 8823

At least, Dylan thought, there was this small comfort: The
saurians, whatever else they might be or might be thinking
about having a smooth-skin in command, were definitely a
professional and efficient crew.

Trying not to squirm in a command chair that was made for
a scaled saurian body, not an unarmored human one, he found
himself, despite the discomfort to his rump, working together
with his odd crew as if they'd always been a team. He and they
together maneuvered the alternate *Andromeda* warily but steadily
on out through the swirling, ever-changing field of space
anomalies without a single incident.

"Open space," the alternate Rommie announced at last.

There was an audible sigh of relief from everyone, saurian and human, on the Command Deck.

"Well done, everyone," Dylan said, for the instant actually forgetting that this wasn't his normal crew.

And in that one instant of mutual satisfaction in a job perfectly done, it seemed that the saurians had also forgotten that he was a smooth-skinned human.

Then Bekha muttered, almost grudgingly, "He doesss seem to know v'hat he doesss." And then the saurian spoiled that almost-compliment by adding, "For a smooth-skin, that isss."

That apparently casual afterthought brought Dylan back to himself with a shock. *No easy assumptions*, he warned himself. *Parallel ship or not, you know nothing about them.*

And once again he was very much aware of being the only human among five (and, for all he knew, more) clawed, muscular, green-scaled saurians. Now that they were out of immediate danger, Dylan told himself, he'd better continue to keep himself essential personnel aboard this ship, at least until he could figure out how to get back to his own dimension.

That means, first of all, that I've got to get myself some decent status here. And that *means I can't risk letting any insults go unchallenged.*

When in doubt, bluff. Having a working knowledge of Tyr's personality was really coming in handy in this place. Now Dylan took on the role of Tyr at the Nietzschean's most coldly and dangerously logical.

"Bekha," he declared, ice fairly crackling from the words,

"like it or not, we are stuck together on this ship. And whether you like it or not, I am your captain. And as your captain, I will *not* tolerate any further sniping at me or at anyone else of this crew. Is that understood?"

He paused for a split second, then, when Bekha said nothing, repeated, voice even more forceful and fierce, "I asked you a question and you will answer me! *Is that understood?*"

Bekha hissed softly at that, but did not meet his gaze.

All right, he'd take that as an apology. He really wasn't eager to jump into a fight with these folks.

Whoa, wait a minute. Now that Dylan had a moment's peace in which to think about it, there was something missing from this scenario. In this dimension there didn't seem to be any odd and unidentified enemy fleet shooting at them. Dylan didn't exactly miss them, but he did have to wonder why they hadn't turned up here as well.

Is that difference important?

For that matter, did the fact that they were getting farther and farther away from the point of transfer mean that he wasn't going to be able to get back? Or didn't something as finite as a specific location matter in something that was as vast and fluid as space?

One worry at a time, Dylan told himself. "I assume that while I am aboard this ship, I have a cabin."

"There isss a captain'sss cabin," Tyr snarled. "And it isss reserved only for *our* captain!"

Dylan shook his head in wry wonder. "You are really predictable, you know that?"

"V'hat does that—"

"Don't start arguing about it. You know exactly what I meant by that. All right, all of you, if this ship really is an alternate of my own that means it has only a relatively small crew. And that means that yes, there are certainly going to be plenty of vacant cabins."

Yes, he caught a wince from Bh'em that told him he was right about that. These folks must have suffered through some situation similar to his own.

"I also assume that while I'm here as your surrogate captain," Dylan continued, "I may freely access the shipboard library and any other items that will help me to *be* captain."

In other words, he added silently, *to let me find out more about this ship, this situation, and whatever else I may be facing while I'm here.*

Dylan paused, studying their bony saurian faces and getting absolutely no clues from what he was beginning to realize was their natural lack of expression—couldn't emote too well with that sweep of jawbone—and then went boldly ahead with what he was gambling was the right way to deal with them: with sheer force.

"Be sensible!" Dylan shouted as if suddenly overcome by saurian rage. "What do you think I'm going to do, learn all your weaknesses and use the information to form an invasion army of one? You may not have noticed, what with all your hysterics—yes, I said hysterics!—but I am the only 'smooth-skin' on board. Your captain and I changed places, period. There are no invasion forces on either side, just two Dylan Hunts. Do you get that? Yes?"

"So now, *as* Captain Dylan Hunt, the only captain that you've got right now, glottal stops and clicks notwithstanding, you are going to give me a cabin, and *you will let me access that shipboard library.*"

By God, it worked again. He could practically feel the hostility all around him, and the contempt. But no one even tried to stop him.

No?

Tyr'h leaped up from his spot without so much as a tensed muscle in warning, did an amazing leap straight up, twisted lithely in midair, agilely bounded off a wall, feet first, twisted again in midair, and landed lightly on his feet again to confront Dylan, blocking his way.

Oh hell. Just like my Tyr, augmented for speed and reaction time. Probably augmented for strength, too. "Deft of you," Dylan drawled, refusing to show his growing alarm. "Let me guess, you're not going to let me pass."

"Clever, smooth-skin."

"I *said* that you were predictable. And now, of course, your next step is going to be to challenge me."

"You dare to mock me!"

"Actually, no, I'm not mocking you, I'm just stating what seems pretty obvious to me. And here's another pretty obvious bit: You're not going to listen to reason, are you? Such as, this ship does need a captain, and as I said before, right now I'm the only one you've got.

"No," he added, seeing the saurian tense, "I guess you're not going to listen at all."

The classic situation, yep, fight or flight, no way around it. Flight was, under the circumstances, not an option. Particularly, Dylan thought, since there really wasn't anywhere to go. Even if he was foolish enough to try to make a run for it.

The rest of the crew was watching the confrontation with cold, calm, almost analytical interest. Dylan really doubted that their kind liked losers. Was this a prearranged fight worked out by some subtle signals that he hadn't caught? Or were they all simply bored or fed up with the routine of shipboard life and hungry for any sort of new entertainment?

Such as, perhaps, the pleasures of watching one of their warriors demolish a smooth-skin.

Sorry to disappoint you, folks. I may look like a "smooth-skin," but I'm not that much of a pushover.

But fight wasn't such a great option, either. No weapons but bare hands against a saurian armed with claws. No armor but skin and clothes against a saurian with natural armor. And, just to add to the problem facing him, said saurian had cat-like speed and agility.

Not good.

He and Tyr'h circled warily, the traditional opening move for any fight, each one waiting for the other to strike. Watching the saurian reflexively flex his claws, Dylan refused to let himself be intimidated. But even so, he knew that one mistake would mean that Tyr'h would casually rip him open.

Not a chance of it, guy.

Dylan took a shot at it and lunged first. Tyr'h slid sideways, and Dylan's own momentum carried him helplessly forward. But he was used to sparring against Tyr's greater speed. Dylan tucked his head under and turned his helpless lunge into a forward roll, narrowly missing having his back torn by saurian claws but landing neatly back on his feet. He whirled—

Just in time to meet the impact of Tyr'h's flattened hand. Fortunately, it was a glancing blow or it would have broken bones, but it still hit home with enough force to send Dylan staggering back, struggling to focus and feeling as though his brain was rattling about in his skull.

Come on, damn it, he told himself, *snap out of it!* Move!

The saurian moved first, launching a high kick that connected with Dylan's chest. Dylan went flying backward, crash-landing flat on his back with a force that drove the wind from him. He lay gasping for breath for a few moments, wondering if ribs had been cracked.

Doesn't matter. Can't just lie here.

As Tyr'h leaped, claws extended, Dylan brought his legs up and kicked up and out with as much force as he could muster. He hit the saurian full in the chest, and sent Tyr'h tumbling over backwards. But what should have been a helpless fall turned into a quick, graceful backflip and twist that brought the saurian instantly back on his feet and facing Dylan.

Oh, now that's just not right!

Dylan had just enough time to get back on his feet himself before Tyr'h came at him again. Those deadly claws swept sideways, ripping through Dylan's shirt and scoring the skin underneath.

Hell!

At least the saurian hadn't gotten in a clean swipe. Dylan could feel the blood already starting to trickle down his chest, tickling, but knew it was nothing worse than scratches. He might not be so lucky next time.

Can't let there be *a next time. But, damn it all to Magog hell, he's wiping up the deck with me!*

Wait, wait, if he'd learned one thing from Tyr, other than frustration and downright fury, it was that anything—anything at all—could be used as a weapon. Such as . . . such as what?

Whoa, wait . . . think . . .

Oh yes.

Worth a shot. So to speak.

Dylan feinted to the left, to the right, making the saurian react with blazing speed—and yes, sure enough, Tyr'h's very speed worked against him. The laws of physics demanded that if he moved swiftly to the left, weight and balance both all to the left, he couldn't instantly turn that into a move to the right without wrenching even augmented joints. Dylan feinted to the left again, and for a split second his target was open—

Yes! Dylan brought his knee up with all his force, aiming right at the most vulnerable spot in a man—

Got him!

It was clearly a vulnerable spot in a saurian, too. Tyr'h doubled up with an agonized hiss, clutching himself. Dylan finished the job with a linked-fist rabbit punch, putting all his strength behind it, on the back of Tyr'h's neck.

Damn, that hurt! Those scales made it feel as if he'd just punched armor. But Tyr'h hadn't fallen, so Dylan, gritting his teeth, hit him again, once more with all his force.

At first he was sure that, even so, Tyr'h, gasping and doubled over, struggling for breath but stubbornly still on his feet, wasn't going to fall.

Then all at once, with a final whoosh of air, the saurian collapsed in a most satisfying heap and didn't get up.

I was right, Dylan thought, standing over him and surreptitiously checking to see that the saurian was still breathing. *Folks covered with all those protective scales wouldn't need to wear pants unless there was something under those pants that was more vulnerable than the rest and worth protecting.*

Struggling not to pant or rub his bruises and scrapes, determinedly ignoring that irritating tickle of blood still trickling down his claw-scratched chest, Dylan asked the other saurians, "Anyone else have any problems?"

No, they clearly did not. No one moved even the slightest bit forward. But no one rushed to help Tyr'h, either.

"Now," Dylan said flatly, "I am going to my cabin." *To a cabin, at any rate.*

When no one made so much as the slightest move to tell him where it might be, Dylan gave a mental shrug: He'd figure it out for himself, since a parallel *Andromeda* couldn't have *that* foreign a layout.

"And," Dylan added, looking down at his shredded shirt and sweaty, scratched-up, bruised, and bloody self, "I am also going to whatever passes for a shower and clean clothes!"

FIVE • QUESTIONS AND SOME ANSWERS

Two things worry most people these days.
One: that things may never get back to normal.
And two: that they already have.
—LARIS STEN, INTERSTELLAR PHILOSOPHER,
RAMBLINGS AND RECORDINGS, CV 4151

Unchallenged, Dylan left the Command Deck.

Unchallenged, he did locate a row of cabins, pretty much where their equivalents would be on his ship.

And, unchallenged, he selected a cabin for himself at what was not quite random—since what he actually did was choose the only one of the line of cabins that had a door that actually "agreed" to open for him.

Dylan's next challenge was to figure out how to lock the door behind him. It was a job that should have been simple, but turned out not to be, since the lock had been made for clawed hands, not for relatively stubby human fingers. Finally managing to get the blasted thing to work and feeling at least a little more secure, Dylan turned to look about the cabin.

There was nothing at all alarming. In fact, this looked pretty much like the standard issue for a shipboard cabin for almost any biped species. There was a chair and a desk, with a computer console on it that was easily recognizable as such, and what looked like a pile of rough matting in one corner that was probably the bed. Unfortunately, the walls, ceiling, and floor were all a really revolting shade of greenish-yellow.

Either these folks don't see in the same color spectrum as humans do, or else they have truly lousy taste.

Well, their interior design wasn't important; he could ignore the color scheme easily enough.

An alcove led to what Dylan assumed were sanitary facilities for saurians—either that, he thought wryly, or inquisition devices—and, wonder of wonders, a tiny sonic shower. Of course the force of it was set for saurian scales, but Dylan was able to alter the force so that it wouldn't blast the skin off his bones. Although he hardly felt safe enough to shower even with a locked cabin door, the temptation of being clean again was just too great to be resisted. Dylan gladly got rid of sweat and blood, as well as managing to ease sore muscles a little. No one bothered him, and if someone was spying on the naked smooth-skin, well, that was his/her/its issue.

Nothing to use as a shirt, but hey, in this heat, having to go bare-chested wasn't going to be a problem. If the saurians were offended by the sight of so much scaleless skin, too bad.

Ah, and look, here was a pair of clean trousers that actually almost fit. Life was definitely looking up.

Now, to see if he couldn't access some files . . .

Dylan perched uncomfortably on the chair that had been made for a saurian, and did his best to access the ship's computer via a system that had been made for clawed fingers.

"State name and rank," a flat voice demanded.

"Captain Dylan Hunt."

"Name not recognized."

Whoops, of course not. "Captain Dylahn Huun't," he said instead, trying to mimic the pronunciation as closely as possible.

"Acknowledged."

Ha, got it.

Finding the right file was another matter. If he hadn't known that he could understand the spoken saurian language, he would have thought this was some alien script. But then, written languages, including English, often did differ from the spoken ones, sometimes greatly. A flash of memory reminded him of . . . yes, that was it. This did look more like the old-fashioned Gothic script than anything else, with each letter stiffly and ornately designed.

But he could puzzle out . . . something about this ship . . . interesting, very interesting, if he was reading it correctly . . .

Something suddenly rasped and kept right on rasping. Startled, Dylan looked wildly about, trying to locate the source of the sound, wondering if it meant trouble, something overloading, something about to explode—and then gave a little sigh of relief and a rueful grin at himself. The noise was nothing but a rough beeping coming from what looked pretty close in design to the communication links on his version of *Andromeda*.

He pressed the lit button, and said, "Dylan Hunt here."

"You v'hish to know v'hat differencesss there are between your dimension and oursss." That was definitely Bh'em's voice. "So do I v'hish to learn more about yoursss."

Dylan hesitated a moment, and then shrugged to himself. "Sounds only fair. Where do you want to meet? On the Command Deck?"

I doubt it. We can't speak openly there.

Sure enough, Bh'em countered, "No. We may best speak in a council room." The name the saurian gave it meant nothing to Dylan, but he recognized which room it was by the description.

"I'll be there shortly," Dylan said.

Even as he said that, though, the computer screen's image wavered and then went blank. Coincidence?

Sure it is, Dylan thought, *and I'm a little pink Martian. Bh'em knew exactly where and even when to find me.*

They didn't want him to access those files. Why not? Could be an embarrassing question. He'd seen just enough to wonder if maybe these guys had something to hide from the home office.

"I'll be right there," he amended.

Bh'em was waiting for him in the council room, which was the same disgusting greenish-yellow as everything else but which featured recognizable chairs and a table of smooth . . . wood? A woodlike material, at any rate. Bh'em was sitting in one of the chairs, curled up almost like a saurian Buddha and looking like the very essence of green-scaled serenity. He gestured at Dylan.

"Come, sit, now."

"Let me guess," Dylan began, settling as best he could into a chair not made for human rumps and leaning on the table. "You people know all about the Nietzschean movement and maybe even something about Mr. Troublemaking Friedrich Nietzsche himself."

Bh'em uncurled. "Thisss isss a smooth-skin concept!"

"Then you do know about him!"

"Bah."

"Never mind the literary critique. Nietzsche may have been a smooth-skin in this dimension as well, but I think you *do* know something about his concepts."

"V'he do not borrow ideasss from smooth-skinsss. It isss they who steal ideas from usss."

"Of course they do," Dylan drawled. "I know all about that idea. There used to be an empire called the Soviet Union, and where and when it was isn't important. But they claimed that *they* had invented everything."

Bh'em straightened. "Do you say that I lie?"

"Wouldn't dream of it. Come, let's talk."

Let's talk without giving away too much about my dimension, just in case.

Heh. Not that I could tell you how to get there anyhow.

As Dylan carefully exchanged information with Bh'em, who was being just as wary, he began to see more and more parallels between their two dimensions and the dimensions' histories. . . .

"The Alliance," Bh'em began, "v'hasss a vast network of planetsss, one that stretched across six galaxiesss, all of it united by v'hat is now known asss Slipstream technology."

"So far, so similar," Dylan said, "even to calling it Slipstream. Only in my dimension, we called it the Commonwealth, not the Alliance."

"That isss a minor point."

"Agreed. Please, continue. In my dimension, some were discontented with the Commonwealth." That sounded suitably vague.

"Here, too, it v'hasss so. Call it v'hat you v'hish, soon enough v'he of the saurian kind came to disagree with the Allianss and itsss methodsss."

"Ah."

Dylan thought he saw where this was leading. They'd just come across what was definitely a major change between the histories of their two dimensions. Instead of the "smooth-skinned" Nietzscheans who had arisen in his dimension, here it was these green-scaled saurians who had become the über-warriors. Not the same thing, not at all.

"It took decadesss," Bhe'm continued, "for the saurian kind to grow sufficiently discontented for so major a decision asss must be made. But that discontent grew stronger over the decadesss."

"Let me guess. If your timeline follows the path that I think that it did, it was your saurian kind who had colonies that lay near the Alliance's frontier."

"Yesss. V'he did indeed have colony v'horldsss, and they

v'here, indeed, near that accursed frontier. But even though v'he v'here of the Alliance, it v'hasss *my people*, and my people alone who had to constantly hold the front line against any and all enemy invasionsss."

The enemy being the Magog, Dylan assumed, or at least their analogs in this dimension.

"And it was your saurian people, then," he said, "and not the Nietzscheans of my dimension, who got pretty tired of having to keep defending the frontier"—*to protect your interests*—*no, better be more politic than that*—"to protect your colony worlds and their inhabitants."

"Indeed it v'hasss so. And it v'hasss v'he who finally decided that the Alliance had grown too soft and decadent to survive. Even as those foolsss began making their desperate and pathetic peace treatiesss with their enemiesss, so did v'he begin to make our secret and deadly preparationsss."

"For war."

"V'he did v'hat must be done," Bh'em said flatly. "V'he saw the v'heaknesss, evaluated it, and then moved to remove that v'heaknesss. But in your dimension, it v'hasss different?"

"Oh, not that different. We had a war, too." He gave a brief summary of it, the Nietzscheans against the Commonwealth, too evenly matched for a true victory on either side, then ended with the tragic conclusion, that mutual destruction that had led to the new Dark Ages.

"Unfortunate," was all that Bh'em said when he'd finished.

"Now there's an understatement! Suppose you tell me what happened in this dimension."

"It isss simple. Unlike the . . . misfortune that occurred in your dimension, in thisss one, the saurian kind v'hon our v'har against the Alliance—and v'hon it with honor and relative eassse."

"Ah."

"Because of our successs," Bh'em continued, "no age of darknesss followed that gloriousss victory. Instead, there came a gloriousss age for all saurian kind. It v'hasss a time of v'his-dom, of art, of continuing conquest."

Yeah, right, Dylan thought. *Let's stress that continuing con-quest, shall we?*

It was rather, he corrected silently, a time of the saurian forces gradually taking over other worlds, that was what that glorious age probably contained, including them like neat cogs into one enormous, cold-blooded machine. That machine, of course, included that one colony world, formerly called Earth, of "smooth-skins," humans, who were now reduced to being a servile race.

Not Pax Romana, Dylan thought grimly. *No Roman Peace here. Call it, rather, Pax Sauriana.*

"Then that's what you're doing out here," he said, very care-fully. "Hunting for new worlds to," *force into*, he thought but did not say, settling politically for, "add to your empire."

"V'he do v'hat isss best," Bh'em answered evasively. "Come, v'he should return to the Command Deck."

Dylan raised a skeptical eyebrow. Why the sudden evasive-ness? Was this ship on an espionage mission? That was always possible, though these folks seemed hardly the sort to keep a low profile. It seemed more likely that this was a scouting mission. That would explain why there was only the one ship—unless, of course, there was a whole fleet flying somewhere lost on the other side of the anomaly zone.

But a scouting mission for whom? The saurian empire? Or . . .

There'd been that one tantalizing bit of data in the computer file. Now Dylan mentally reviewed it again. Risky to misjudge this. But . . . what if this ship was, just possibly, part of a breakaway movement from the saurian empire? Maybe even part of an outright rebellion?

That was definitely a bit too risky to voice aloud. After all, the saurians knew perfectly well that they had no real proof that they needed to keep Dylan alive if they were to get their own captain back. And Dylan knew without any false pride just how difficult it had been to flatten Tyr'h; he was going to wear those scratches and bruises for days. Taking on all five saurians at once? No. You only saw a lone, unarmed hero win out against five stronger, bigger, faster foes in the vids.

And call it what these people might, deny it though Bh'em might, what ruled the saurians was still awfully close to the ideals of the Nietzschean movement, from the concept of selective breeding to the body and mind augmentation. All of it was evident in the casual arrogance of these folks, and in the fact that no one, not even Tyr'h, minded that Dylan had won the duel through what humans might call dirty fighting. There was no such concept as "dirty fighting" among the utterly pragmatic Nietzscheans, who believed simply and efficiently in fighting to win.

Asking Nietzschean types such as these saurians if they were spies, or if they'd turned against their sworn allegiance to their empire, was a sure way to get into another fight, or maybe even be killed outright.

What really bothered Dylan, though, as he and Bh'em returned to the Command Deck, was the way that no one quite met his gaze whenever the "smooth-skins" were mentioned by anyone.

What's going on here?

Were the saurians embarrassed just to be stuck here on their ship with one—or could they be avoiding the gaze of some prospective prey? Dylan found himself growing happier with every word and every evasive and not very subtle look away from him that there was no way for these folks to figure out where his dimension lay or to pay it a visit.

It's bad enough for us to have to deal with the aftermath of all the destruction that "our" Nietzscheans caused! We don't need to deal with an invasion from these folks as well.

And he wasn't too thrilled about being even the temporary captain of a people who kept humans enslaved.

This isn't your rightful place or dimension, Dylan warned himself. *You can't get involved.*

Yeah. Too bad I can't make myself believe that.

But he couldn't help but feel that Bh'em had left something out of his proud recitation of saurian conquest. Something, in fact, that seemed to be almost . . . embarrassing to the saurian.

All right, get it out in the open.

"What didn't you tell me?" Dylan asked. "And don't try to pretend it's nothing. It concerns the smooth-skins, too, doesn't it? What's the matter, aren't they being properly subservient?"

"There isss nothing to discusss."

"Really? Then why won't you—"

"There isss nothing to discusss."

Now, I have to wonder about this. Can it be that the humans are rising up against the empire, too?

Dylan sat back, considering his options—which he had to admit weren't all that great. Curiosity about this dimension was not going to get him anywhere but into trouble. And he didn't need to know what was happening here, when it came right down to it. He just needed to stay here long enough for the dimension-transfer to take place again.

"All right, then," Dylan said, decided, "I'm not going to push you. There's something far more important than the politics of your and my dimension right now, and that's straightening everything out and getting your captain back and me returned to my own ship.

"And for that, we need to return to the anomaly zone."

"No!" Bekha snapped.

"It isss foolish to return to danger v'hithout a just cause," Tyr'h added with a teethbaring snarl.

"Oh, there's a just cause, all right," Dylan said. "Or do you not want to have your captain back again?"

Bh'em, whom Dylan had already pegged as being the most logical thinker of the lot, particularly after their private conversation, said after only the briefest of pauses, "Yesss. V'he definitely v'hish our captain back. To be rid of you and have the greatest chanccce of him returning, it seemsss only a logical decision that v'he must, indeed, return to the same location. To asss closely asss isss possible, at any rate."

What Bekha muttered at that decision needed no translation. But with Dylan and Bh'em in agreement, the others slowly agreed as well, and the grumbling saurian was outnumbered. As the ship sped back toward the anomaly zone, though, Bekha continued to all but radiate disgust.

Live with it, Dylan thought.

"V'he have a problem," the Rommie-analog said suddenly.

Hell, now what? "What's wrong?" Dylan asked.

"See for yourselvesss."

An image formed on the command deck's central viewscreen—an image of perfectly normal, perfectly tranquil space.

"V'hat isss this?" Bh'em cried. "V'here isss the anomaly zone? Have you let yourself go off-courssse?"

"I do not do that!" the ship protested. "These are the right coordinatesss. But I cannot find any disturbancesss."

"Check your coordinates again," Dylan ordered.

"I do not make mistakesss!"

"Check them!"

"Coordinatesss confirmed. They are correct." The ship's voice sounded almost sulky.

"Run a new diagnostic, then. Recalibrate sensors."

"There is no need."

"*Do it!*"

"I have done so. There can be no error. The anomaliesss are gone."

Dylan stared in horror at that vast expanse of undeniably utterly normal space.

He was trapped.

SIX • SMOOTH-SKIN SITUATION

Come bitter rain
And wash from my heart
That saddest of all words—
Home.

—ULATEMPA POETESS,
"SONG OF MY EXILE," CY 9825

Beka bit back a sigh of pure, maddened frustration. She had never imagined she'd ever be admitting something like this, not even to herself. But the truth of it was: God, how she missed Dylan, the right Dylan, the Dylan who, like him or hate him, you could argue with and listen to and sometimes even agree with!

"But we can't just go rushing blindly back into the anomaly zone," she repeated carefully yet again. She refused to let herself shout at the saurian since she'd already learned that shouting at him got her nowhere. "We can't do that, not without knowing a lot more about it. Got it?"

She paused, frowning at him. "Do you? Hello? Do you even understand what I'm saying?"

"No . . ." It was a bare whisper. "Can't . . . think . . ."

Now what? "What do you mean by—"

"Cold . . . too cold. . . ."

And wasn't this just great? Here they were stuck in an unfamiliar sector of space, with mysterious attackers still lurking out there somewhere beyond the range of Rommie's sensors, with a zone of who knew what types of spatial anomalies still too close for comfort, and with a saurian Captain Dylahn Huun't in place of their own Dylan Hunt.

And all that said saurian Dylahn Huun't could do to help them out of this mess was—just huddle in the command chair like an old woman and keep complaining about the cold!

"Beka."

It was Bem's tranquil voice. As she turned angrily to him, he continued softly, "I don't think it's his fault."

"Eh?"

But there was something in Bem's eyes that said, think.

Oh. Wait a minute. Maybe Bem was right at that. This dull-witted behavior was just too out of character for, well, for *any* Dylan, even if this wasn't the right one. There might be a good physiological reason for it.

"Those scales, that saurian body—you think that he's cold-blooded, like a real reptile!"

Bem nodded. "He probably needs warmth if his thought processes are going to keep functioning properly."

"Geez. What next? Rommie," Beka called out, "we're going to have to raise the temperature in here."

"How much, Beka?"

"Make it, oh, thirty-four degrees C."

That would make it pretty warm in here, but not unbearably so. Would it be warm enough, though, for the saurian to start waking up? It had better be. She wasn't going to risk baking herself and the others for his sake.

As the degrees began to rise, the saurian stirred as though struggling to break out of a trance. As the degrees settled into being downright hot, Beka mused that if this didn't work, they were going back down to a sane temperature and to hell with cold-blooded creatures.

After a few inactive moments more, though, Dylahn Huun't uncurled from his huddle, sitting bolt upright in the chair so suddenly that Beka started. "Ah, yesss!" he hissed. "Thisss isss a far more sensible temperature."

"For some of us," Beka said wryly, wiping beading drops of sweat off her forehead. "But never mind that. What about our situation? You *are* aware of it, aren't you?"

"Yesss. I remember v'hat v'hasss happening before I grew too chilled to think clearly thanksss to your ridiculously low shipboard temperature."

"And . . . ?"

"And I agree that before we make any movesss, v'he must have some analysesss of the region."

Stifling a sardonic, *No really? Ooh, how brilliant you are*, Beka reminded herself that the guy had, after all, just come out of the equivalent of a deep sleep, or maybe even a coma. She asked instead, with careful restraint, "Harper?"

His voice sounded its usual cocky self even over the faintly tinny sound of the communications channel. "No problem. Got some analyses done already. I'll get 'em all soon enough." But then he added, with what sounded almost like a verbal shrug, "As much as you can really get something that doesn't want to fit into anything, if that makes any sense."

Beka snorted. "It makes about as much sense as anything else that's happened so far."

"V'he must not v'hait too long," Dylahn Huun't cut in sharply. "V'he *must* chart a course back into the anomaly zone. If there isss ever to be any logical opportunity for me to be returned to my rightful command—"

"And for Dylan to be returned to us," Beka snapped.

"Yesss, yesss, that, too," he agreed without interest. "But v'he must be in the same, or at least the similar, region of space if there isss to be even a remotely reasonable chance of such a transfer happening."

His arrogant, so sure-of-itself voice was beginning to grate on Beka's nerves. "You know this for a fact?"

She'd struck a nerve by questioning him. Dylahn Huun't sprang from the chair in sudden ferocity, eyes blazing. "I am the captain! Do you challenge me?"

He towered over her, a great, muscular green-scaled saurian

threat, triggering ancient instincts deep within her that screamed, *Run!*

But Beka never flinched. Waving a sharp hand in warning at the others—*don't move*—she retorted just as fiercely, staring straight into those hot eyes, "Do you want to get back to your ship again or not?"

It was like facing down Tyr at his most arrogant. Assuming, of course, that Tyr had somehow sprouted claws and greenish scales.

Boy, I don't want to think about how these guys advance through the ranks, Beka thought. *Must be blood and body parts all over the ship. Those claws aren't just for show.*

Yes, she added to herself, *but they have to have some self-control or they'd never be able to crew a ship together. They're not mindless Magog.*

Her gamble paid off. Sure enough, just as Tyr might suddenly see the logic of a situation over raw anger, so did the saurian suddenly seem to deflate back to his merely normally tall self. He sat back down in the command chair, arrogant pride still in every line. But the saurian admitted after a bare instant of silence, "I do not know for a fact that v'he must be there, but there isss, logically, nothing elssse to be done."

"Unfortunately," Rommie cut in suddenly, her image forming beside Beka, "Captain Huun't is right. While there's little accurate data to be found, what little there is indicates that yes, we really do stand a better chance of an exchange taking place when we are back in the anomaly zone."

Beka sighed. "I was afraid that you were going to say that.

All right, then, everyone, you heard Rommie. Looks like we're going back into the proverbial lion's mouth."

That earned her equally blank stares from Dylahn Huun't, Tyr, Trace, and Bem, and a "Huh?" over the comm from Harper.

Beka sighed. "It's an old Earth idiom, something from a circus act, I think, meaning, roughly, um, deliberately putting yourself into danger."

"Circus?" Trance asked.

Rommie recited, "Circus: the word from the old Earth Latin *circus*, or circle, originating in the First Millennium BC, old style count, Roman Empire, and meaning a form of entertainment to be found in many cultures, in particular human cultures, and generally featuring acts of skill and comedy, formerly featuring acts of human death, particularly in the heyday of the Roman Empire, but now more likely to include animal performances of herbivores or carnivores, performances on high wires, various acrobatics—"

"Call it entertainment," Beka summarized hastily.

"Lion?" Dylahn Huun't asked.

That's the last time I use an old Earth idiom, I swear it.

Before Rommie could begin another lengthy definition, Beka told them all, with great control, "A lion was an old Earth predator. Big cat, big mouth, long fangs. Got it? Then let's get going.

"And," she added, unable to resist completing the thought, "let's just hope that the lion isn't hungry."

Since they weren't in any immediate state of crisis, and hopefully wouldn't be for a while, Beka took the chance to leave the Command Deck for a brief break, and take a few moments to stretch her legs a little.

She was striding enthusiastically halfway down a corridor, working the kinks out of her arms as well as she went, glad of the chance to move, when an unmistakable growl behind her said, "Beka."

"Tyr." With great reluctance, Beka turned to look up at him, not really wanting to get into an argument with him right now. "What's wrong?"

"You know what's wrong." His face was grim, his eyes twin black stones. "Him—that creature you've left in command."

"Not in command. Just in the command chair. Our good Rev will keep him under control."

"Yes, yes, he'll try. But we can't trust him."

"Who? Bem?"

"Don't joke with me, Beka. You know who I mean—that cold-blooded green-scaled lizard."

Beka gritted her teeth to hold back what she really wanted to snap at him, which was something short, sharp, and reflecting on his ancestry. "No," she said with great restraint. "I don't trust the saurian. He's an alien from who knows what dimension, with who knows what kind of a personal history. But for all that, he *is* an alternate Dylan. And whatever else he may be, that means that there have got to be *some* similarities between the two of them."

"Such as?"

"Well. A sense of honor, for one thing."

"Bah. What honor can a lizard know?"

"He could ask the same of us: What honor can a monkey know?"

With that, Beka continued with her brisk walk, adding over her shoulder, "And since he's a captain of another Rommie, and a sentient being, I'd say that it's also a pretty safe bet that what this guy wants most of all is the same thing that our own Dylan wants: to just get home."

Tyr moved smoothly forward with Nietzschean speed to block her way. "I can't accept that."

She stood her ground. "Really? And what would you do?"

"Not give him the command chair, that's for certain!"

"What do you want me to do with him?" Beka asked impatiently. "Slap him in the brig?"

"Well?"

"Look, Tyr, you heard the whole thing. Rommie and I both think that we've got to keep to the parallel situations, including captain and command chair, as closely as possible if we're going to get Dylan back."

"And . . . are we so eager to get him back?"

That brought her up short, staring at Tyr. *Were* they?

"Well?" Tyr prodded again.

What Beka finally said was said as much to convince herself as it was for him. "Tyr, personal feelings don't have anything to do with this. If we lost one Dylan and got one Dylan in exchange, that seems to say, at least to me, that there's some kind of cosmic balance, mass and energy and all that, between dimensions, and it's a balance that needs to be kept. No choice about it: We have to get our Dylan back again."

She turned and headed swiftly back toward the Command Deck before this could go any further, aware that Tyr was following so closely he was nearly treading on her heels. "First we get our Dylan back," Beka told them both, "and *then* we worry about what to do about him."

It wasn't turning out to be all that easy to deal with this alternate captain. For one thing, Beka thought, even at his most frustratingly honorable, Dylan had never been so incredibly, utterly maddeningly *stubborn*.

"But we *can't* just go straight ahead!" Beka all but shouted at their surrogate captain.

He glared at her. "And v'hy not?"

"Are you blind? Those—those—that crazy spatial distortion's going to tear us apart!"

"V'he can do it," the saurian snapped. "That isss the best v'hay back to v'here v'ere v'hen this nonsense happened!"

"I don't advise it," Rommie's voice cut in, filled with her most inhuman calmness. "I would stand a reasonably good chance of surviving the encounter with so many bizarre stresses—at least so I believe without my having made further calibrations to prove the point—but you almost certainly wouldn't. I really don't want to lose another crew."

"There!" Beka said in triumph. "Did you hear that? Rommie thinks it's impossible, too!"

"V'he can do it," the saurian repeated, "and survive. There isss nothing to be gained by cowardiccce."

"Cowardice!"

"It isn't cowardice to avoid something dangerous," Trance said simply. "It's merely good sense."

The saurian ignored her. "Do you v'hish your captain back again or not?" he roared.

"Of course we do," Rev Bem said calmly. "But we also want to be alive to greet him. Perhaps your species is better able to endure the spatial stresses—"

"Ha, yesss, smooth-skins are v'heak!"

"I am not weak!" Tyr roared. "And I've had enough of this garbage!"

He lunged in one incredibly smooth Nietzschean move. The saurian leaped up from the command chair like a launched missile, and he and Tyr crashed together with an impact that reminded Beka of two boulders smashing together. The force of it sent them both crashing sideways onto the floor.

"Oh hell," Beka said helplessly, watching them wrestle. Aware that Bem had moved to her side, she asked over her shoulder, "What d'you think, Bem? Shoot them both?"

"That *would* be a properly Nietzschean solution."

"Yeah. Too bad that I'm not a Nietzschean."

The saurian and Nietzschean continued to silently grapple on the floor, evenly matched for strength, speed, and ferocity, with those sharp saurian claws raking futilely against the metal mesh of Tyr's vest.

Beka shook her head. Sooner or later, one of them was going to run out of energy, or make a mistake. How were they going to get out of this ridiculous show of, well, testosterone and whatever passed for testosterone in a saurian, without any serious damage to anyone?

Then a sudden inspiration hit her, so hard that Beka nearly laughed out loud. Damn it, yes! She murmured, "Rommie?"

Rommie's image instantly materialized next to her, eyebrows raised in interest. "Yes?"

"We still do have full tanks of fire extinguishing gel on board, don't we?"

"Yes. Of course we do."

Every spaceworthy ship carried firefighting materials on every deck and in every cabin. A shipboard fire in deep space was one of the major terrors in the mind of every spacer. In the confined area of a ship, with oxygen within and a vacuum without, there'd be no escape. A fire would quickly turn into a deadly firestorm.

Beka grinned. "Well, Rommie? Go ahead and extinguish the fire, if you would."

"The . . . fire?" Then Rommie understood and gave a very human grin back at her. "Ah. Indeed."

Without warning, a foaming, frothing mass of white gel poured down on the two fighters, burying them. Even two such determined beings as they had to give up when they ran out of air. After a few minutes of the gel roiling and heaving like a monstrous living thing, they both struggled free on opposite sides of the white mound, coughing and spitting out gel.

"What the *hell*!" Tyr got out.

The saurian hissed out something equally hot in his language.

"I'm so sorry, gentle, ah, beings," Beka said sweetly. "Your fighting was so hot that it must have somehow set off a fire detector."

As they both swore at her, she—simply smiled. Funny, this: For all the swearing, neither of them offered to start fighting again.

Peace.

For the moment.

SEVEN • CAPTAIN SMOOTH-SKIN

Never settle with words that which can be more
effectively accomplished with heavy artillery.

—NIETZSCHEAN PROVERB

Dylan realized suddenly that he'd been staring fiercely at the
viewscreen at that undisturbed region of space like a kid back
on old Earth wishing for Santa Claus to arrive, watching for
the anomaly zone to reappear.

A watched zone never appears, he thought wryly.

Fortunately for his already dubious status among them, the
saurians were all just as stunned, just as busy staring.

Come on, guy, do something! Dylan prodded himself. *There
has to be something, some clue that you're missing, that* we're
missing. . . .

If this was his own *Andromeda,* there wouldn't be any problem. Seamus Harper would already be on the case. That wise-cracking nuisance of a genius would already be hunting for everything from altered star patterns—hey!—no, that was out, as blatant as that would already have been noticed. But Harper would be hunting for even the smallest quarks out of place, or the traces of—

Traces?

As in emanations?

All right, yes! An idea had finally hit him!

"Rommie—" No, wait, here her name was . . . um . . . Rhom'hai, yes, that was it, and maybe he'd get that glottal stop right this time. "Rhom'hai," ha, yes, he'd gotten it right. "I want you to widen your search spectrum. Go after every frequency you can reach. Do a sweep. Anomalies as large and violent as those are definitely going to leave some kind of traces, of emanations of some sort, behind."

"And if we find them?" Bh'em asked. "V'hat then? Do v'he just sit and v'hait like meek little dweti-birdsss, hoping that the anomaliesss politely return?"

"No," Dylan countered, "we keep watch on those traces and see if they're fading or increasing in intensity."

"Ahhh! Clever!" It was a grudging admission. "If they increasse, then it must mean only the one logical thing: the anomaliesss are cyclical in nature, not merely singularitiesss, and really are going to return!"

And if they decrease, that means that they're almost certainly gone for good, and my proverbial goose is cooked, Dylan finished silently. He'd already established himself as a trouble-making smooth-

skin. If these folks wouldn't be able to get their rightful captain back, they would have no reason to keep him alive. *How
many, I wonder, can I take out before they get me?*

Not exactly a comforting thought.

The ship was silent for a disconcertingly long while. The
saurians all sat like green-scaled statues, and Dylan sat as still
as he could, even though his heart was racing at what felt like
light speed.

"Analyzing spectrum 1K59D," Rhom'hai said suddenly.
"No tracesss found. Analyzing spectrum 1K60D. No tracesss
found."

The list went on for some time, and Dylan began to doubt
himself. Hell, what if he was wrong?

No, that didn't make any sense. Maybe he wasn't some wizkid genius like Harper, but even he knew enough about interstellar physics to know that a zone that large and active had to
leave *some* emanations behind.

"Analyzing spectrum 10M46E," the ship continued mechanically. "No tracesss found. Analyzing spectrum 10M47E.
No tracesss found. Analyzing spectrum 10M48E—trace
found."

Dylan sat bolt upright. "Say that again."

"That spectrum does show tracesss of—" Rhom'hai rattled
off a series of incomprehensible syllables that were presumably the names of some of the more obscure elements. When
neither Dylan nor any of the saurians replied—the saurians
looked downright baffled, in fact—Rhom'hai added in explanation, "They are quite a unique combination of trace ele-

mentsss to find in normal space, but the combination is compatible v'hith those that v'here emitted by the anomaly zone."

Dylan struggled to keep his voice absolutely calm. "Now do an analysis to see if the traces are strengthening or weakening."

"Preliminary analysisss does indicate that they are . . ."

"Are? Are what?"

Instead of answering, Rhom'hai announced in a voice that rang out as loudly and clearly as a war trumpet, "Enemy shipsss approaching! Squadron of five! Enemy shipsss approaching!"

The announcement brought the saurians to their feet, hissing in a mix of anger and alarm.

Oh, there's a great way to meet a challenge! Dylan thought sourly. "Return to your stations!" he snapped. "That is an order! *Return to your stations!*"

Well, what did you know? They actually obeyed.

Dylan's first thought was that this rapidly approaching fleet must be this dimension's version of the strangers who'd attacked his *Andromeda* back in his dimension. "Rhom'hai. Give us more data."

Rhom'hai announced in a slightly more normal tone, "They are undeniably *Tregarth'k*-classs."

The saurians fell instantly, deathlessly, still.

Not strangers after all, Dylan thought. "You know these ships!" he snapped. "Come on, everyone, give me some information! This is a familiar enemy, isn't it? Damn it, don't get coy with me now!" he added at everyone's sudden hesitation. "Who are they?"

"Armed as we are," Bh'em said shortly.

"What are you telling me? That we're going to be attacked by your own people? Yes, that fits: You all nearly jumped out of your skins when Rhom'hai identified the ships."

Bekha muttered, "They're sending a message."

"Let's hear it."

"We don't need it."

"I'm getting awfully tired of this nonsense. *I said, let's hear it!*"

With a snarl, Bheka opened the channel.

Sure enough, it was another saurian's face that appeared on the screen. No surprise there. It was obviously someone of importance, which did surprise Dylan a little. Although the saurians, with their bony faces and lack of body hair, didn't show age as humans did, those dark orange eyes were cold and shadowed with what could only be long years of experience.

The officer's voice was so choked with rage it was difficult to understand, but Dylan made out, ". . . traitorsss! Thisss rebellion endsss here and now!"

Rebellion? Dylan echoed silently. *Well, what do you know? I was right. Not that the data does me any good right now!*

Speaking out wasn't going to help the situation: The last thing that furious officer would want to see was a "smooth-skin" on board.

It didn't matter. "They've cut the signal," Behka snapped.

"Not in the mood to parlay, I take it," Dylan said dryly.

"Their v'heaponsss are all online," Rhom'hai commented, "and they are powering up."

"Not in the mood," Dylan answered himself.

No time to think about what that might mean to him and his survival. "All right, you rebels, you know the situation better than me. Tell me just this one thing: Is it fight or flight?"

"Fight!" the saurians thundered back as one.

"Figured as much."

The enemy was coming at them in a wedge formation. That was not the greatest move against a single ship, presenting such an obvious problem for the leading ship in the wedge, and it was really foolish of the enemy to underestimate even a single foe. They presumably believed that these folks would cave in under the superior threat and turn and run.

Like hell they will, Dylan thought. *Damned if I'm going to die over someone else's problem.*

"Battle stations!" he ordered over the open communications link, just in case there actually were other crewmembers elsewhere on the ship. "Arm weapons but do not fire. Repeat, *do not fire!*"

Ty'rh leaped up at that, roaring in fury, "Smooth-skin! You cannot command usss in battle!"

"Sit down!" Dylan roared back at him. "I said, *sit down!* I am your captain, and if you challenge me again," *you'll be a gelding—no, better not say that without a weapon in hand,* "you won't live to pass on your genes!" Yes, that sounded more properly Nietzschean.

It worked, too. Ty'rh actually did settle back down, not quite growling under his breath.

Dylan continued in his best *I am the dictator here* voice to all of the Command Deck crew, "I want to live through this encounter as much as you. And this is hardly the first military engagement I've seen!"

Yes, and hopefully this won't actually become *a military engagement.*

Uh-huh, right, he told himself sardonically, *and all these guys will turn out to be closet vegetarians.*

"They've made a bad mistake," Dylan shouted, "and we're taking advantage of it. Full speed, full ahead! Yes, that's right, that's what I said: *full ahead!* Bekha, be ready for quick maneuvers on my command. *Now!*"

Estimating here from the brief time that it generally took his *Andromeda* to fire, they had only two seconds before the first enemy blast—ha, yes, here it came. But they were already moving so swiftly that the blasts missed them completely, and now they were aimed like a missile straight at the bow of the lead ship—

The wedge broke up into five ships desperately trying to get out of this lunatic's way. No time for the enemy to fire, no room for them to fire without hitting their own ships. But *Androom'da* and her crew were under no such restraints. As Bekha kept the ship diving and rolling through the ever-moving maze of enemies, Dylan ordered, "Fire at will!"

They could hardly miss at this range. One blast took out an enemy's engine. Two ships trying to avoid that explosion collided—

Oh Lord, this isn't going to be pretty "Get us out of here, *fast!*" Dylan ordered.

Sure enough, the two colliding ships exploded, and sure enough, that triggered a chain reaction of new explosions across the remaining vessels. Even as *Androom'da* sped away, the shockwave of the final enormous blast hit the ship and sent them tumbling end over end. Bekha, snarling, clung to the console, fighting the controls, somehow managing to return them to level again and in one piece, but the ship hurtled helplessly through space until the shockwave finally faded away.

"Full stop," Dylan ordered. "Rhom'hai! Scan for enemy ships."

"There are none v'hithin sensor range."

The saurians roared their approval so fiercely that Dylan's ears rang. A wry corner of his mind whispered, *Dylan Hunt, Dinosaur Hunter.*

He ignored it. That chain reaction of explosions was *not* what he had wanted. How could you celebrate having just destroyed five ships of sentient beings?

Yes, but what if the explosions hadn't destroyed them all? He hadn't, after all, seen all five ships die. What if the survivors had gone into Slipstream to escape? The explosions would have hidden any traces of that. And if there were, indeed, survivors, they'd be back, or at the very least delivering words of warning to their superiors.

Damn. Suddenly he felt really dizzy. Dylan blinked, blinked again, and then rubbed a quick hand over his eyes. This was hardly a safe place for a human to show any weakness.

"Rhom'hai," he said, resolutely forcing himself back into the role of the warrior captain, "check for damage."

"I am checking . . . no damage reported."

"Very good. Now get us back to the anomaly traces and re-sume your analysis." Dylan turned in his chair to face Bh'em. "Bh'em, you and I have some serious talking to do. I give you your choice: We either talk in that council room or here and now."

"Do v'he?"

"No games! We just survived a one-against-five battle, and I think I've earned some honest answers."

"There are no secretsss from these people."

"So be it. Now, here's what I think. You, all of you here, are three hundred years out of your time, am I right?"

There, now, the dizziness was easing up.

His announcement made Bh'em start—and then realize that the reaction had given him away. "How did—Ah, you asss v'hell?"

"Me asss v'hell," Dylan mimicked savagely.

"So!" Bh'em exclaimed. "It seemsss that there isss yet an-other parallel between the two of usss."

"Yes, there is." Dylan leaned forward. "Now, tell me this, Bh'em, and please don't start avoiding the question."

"V'hat do you mean?"

"I'm giving you the benefit of the doubt here. I'm assuming that the parallel between us means that you were in the right just now and those guys who attacked us were in the wrong. But I need to be sure about it. So tell me this: What has gone wrong with your society?"

"Nothing!"

"Oh, right," Dylan said in disgust. "Your own people attacked you just for the hell of it."

"They . . ."

"Yeah. It's not so easy to come up with a convincing excuse, is it? Come on, Bh'em, let's have the truth." He gave an angry little bark of a laugh. "Hey, it's not as if I'm going to be able to tell anyone about it!"

"There isss that. Ahhh, but it isss not so easy to discussss." Reluctantly, Bh'em admitted, "After our three hundred yearsss out of time, v'he found that there had been . . . changesss."

"Believe me, I understand that part."

"Heh. Perhapsss you do at that." Bh'em shook his head. "In our rightful time, understand, oursss v'hasss an empire of strength, of honor."

Dylan sighed. "Just as once upon a time I knew a Commonwealth of strength and honor. Amazing how much can change in three hundred years, isn't it?"

Bh'em sighed. "Indeed that isss so. There isss a saying that perhapsss you know: 'All degradesss v'ith time, even the strongessst.' It seemsss to be a true thing. V'hen an empire growsss too large, it isss not such a simple thing to control."

"Granted."

"There isss alwaysss the danger of it losing itself completely."

Oh damn, here came another wave of dizziness. Dylan tried to hide it as best he could.

"Yes," he said, forcing out the words. "That happened to my people in my dimension over and over again in our past history."

"So . . . then you do understand. V'hat v'hasss once a glorious empire can, over time, become instead nothing but a . . . machine made up of little mindsss, mindsss v'hithout courage or honor. Those who still do possesss both courage and honor are forced by it to become nothing but small piecesss of that machine."

"Or else they break away."

There. The dizziness seemed to be fading away again. He really should see about eating or drinking something. Might be low on salt, or protein or something along those lines.

"Or . . . yesss, they break av'hay."

In my dimension, we got that new Dark Ages, Dylan thought. *Here, they got—bureaucrats.*

Not much to choose between, when you came right down to it.

Good Lord, he realized with a shock, *these folks are, in their own predatory way, doing the same thing that I'm doing in my dimension.*

"You really are a ship of rebels," he summarized, "and that's why you're out here alone. You're planning your own new and more honorable empire, aren't you?" Then Dylan added thoughtfully, studying Bh'em. "There's another issue, isn't there?"

"V'hat?"

"It's something more, well, personal, isn't it? No insult

meant, but you don't exactly look like the rest of the crew."

"Smooth-skin, you are too clever."

"For my own good, you mean?" Dylan gave a wry grin. "I've heard that before. But . . . ?"

"But, yesss, yesss, it isss so. I do not look very much like the othersss. That isss because I carry the ancient bloodline of Tah'rat, the priestly line. But here, three hundred yearsss later," he added with a hint of disgust in his voice, "I have found myself to be the only one left of that line."

"What . . . happened?"

"Simply put, the othersss of my line did not look like v'hat the empire hasss now decreed to be the norm."

"Prejudice can be downright deadly," Dylan agreed. Very, very carefully, he added, "Then you can understand why you shouldn't be so swift to look down on the humans as 'smooth-skins.' "

"Hah!"

"But you do see my point."

"Human, you should have been a negotiator."

"Now, why do I get the feeling that I've just been subtly insulted? But think about this, Bh'em: If things have changed so much for you over three hundred years, how much could they have changed for the humans as well?"

"Hah."

Just then, Rhom'hai cut in with, "I sensss more shipsss. And they are rapidly approaching."

EIGHT • STRANGER IN A STRANGE LAND

> Reality is merely an illusion, albeit a very persistent one.
>
> —ALBERT EINSTEIN,
> TWENTIETH-CENTURY EARTH

Captain Dylahn Huun't paused for a moment to delicately pick one last bit of firefighting gel out from under a claw, and then settled himself back onto the command chair. Rommie had already reabsorbed all the firefighting mess that had covered the Command Deck, leaving it as tidy as before.

"Clever," the saurian said with a dip of his head to Beka. "Dousing a . . . fire like that."

There was a *hint* of reluctant humor in his voice. But Beka didn't like the *hint* of coldness that she saw glint in his eyes at the same time. Yes, he had seen the funny side of the situation, but at the same time, Beka had injured his pride, humiliating him like that.

And in front of, what does he call us, smooth-skins as well. Way to go, Beka. "Blessed are the peacemakers"—*hah.*

Tyr hadn't returned to the Command Deck, but hey, that was Tyr all over. He surely had the common sense not to get into another fight in here. Instead, he was probably working off his insulted anger in their improvised gym. Not a problem, Beka thought. She could deal with him. She—more or less—understood him. After all, Nietzschean or not, he was still—again, more or less—human.

"It isss a logical fact," Dylahn Huun't said without warning, as though it were a totally new idea that he'd just discovered. "V'he must not rush blindly into the anomaly zone."

Oh sure, Beka thought, *now* he agreed with them.

Rommie's image suddenly materialized on the viewscreen. "We can't, at any rate."

"V'hat?"

"Even if we did want to blindly rush into the anomaly zone—which of course we don't—there doesn't seem to *be* an anomaly zone right now."

Beka stared at her. "What are you saying, Rommie? It—all that—couldn't have just, well, disappeared!"

"Unfortunately, it could. And apparently has."

"Sure has," came Harper's voice over the open communications link. "I know it's pretty weird, but hey, weird is pretty normal for us. Rommie and I are doing scans right now to see if we can find out where the anomalies went, and I'm also working on my own calculations and analyses. But so far . . ." Only Harper could have managed to give a verbal shrug.

"But so far, the data all seem to say the same thing," Rommie continued. "The anomalies have simply—vanished."

Beka shook her head. "This doesn't make sense. We're talking about a pretty vast segment of space here, not some tiny planetoid. How could something that vast have just vanished?"

"That," Rommie retorted, "is why they are called anomalies."

Beka sat back in her chair with a sigh of utter frustration. For the last . . . well, it seemed as if it had been days, even if the shipboard clock told her, no, it was still shipboard evening of the same day. For almost seven full hours, then, which was long enough for eyestrain and backache to develop, she and the others, including Rommie and Captain Huun't, had been searching everything possible, from trace elements to past records in Rommie's databanks.

"Anything new?" Beka asked wearily.

Even Rommie's voice sounded a little tired. "Something," she said. "I have calculated now that there is a better than eighty-nine percent chance of the anomaly zone reopening."

"And v'hat isss the percentage of that actually happening v'hithin our lifetimesss?" Dylahn Huun't asked, getting to his feet and stretching lithely.

"Seventy-eight percent," Rommie admitted.

"Absolute data, or best essstimate?"

"Estimate."

Beka glanced at the saurian, who was performing a seemingly boneless series of calisthenics, easily bending over backwards in a way that made her merely human spine ache. "Then it could go either way," she said. "All right, then. Let's go with the best case scenario, which says that it reopens in the morning. Whatever happens, Rommie will warn us."

"Of course," Rommie agreed.

Beka smothered a yawn. "Which gives us a chance to get some rest. I assume that even you, Captain Huun't, need sleep."

He straightened. "Indeed."

"There is something else," Rommie added, and Beka turned with a touch of alarm. Now what?

"I have been checking our alternate captain's genetic and chemical makeup," the ship continued, "and we have a small problem."

"V'hat do you mean?" the saurian exclaimed. "V'hat is v'hrong now?"

"You, Captain Huun't, have a slightly different metabolic system from everyone else on board."

"Of course I do! How could I not? You are all smooth-skinsss while I am not!"

"While that description is not exactly scientific, you have hit upon the basic problem: Everyone on board, regardless of his or her species, comes from the same dimension—except for you. You need a certain enzyme that the people of this dimension, or at least those who are my crew, do not metabolize. If you are going to remain at what I suspect you'd call optimum functioning level, you will need it very soon."

"How soon?" Beka asked.

"If he doesn't receive it within a full shipboard day," Rommie returned, "we will have a very sick saurian as our captain."

"That isss impossible!" Captain Huun't protested. "I am in perfect health. I don't feel the slightest trace of sicknesss."

"For now, yes. After a day more in this dimension, it will be otherwise. And after two days . . . we may not be able to do the switch. Also, as we already know, we can't be sure exactly how long it will be until the anomalies reappear and give us any chance at all of returning each captain to his right place."

Beka tensed. "Then *our* Dylan's in trouble, too!"

"It seems likely. We can only assume that the problem has also been noted on Captain Huun't's ship—"

"Of course it hass been noted!" the saurian exclaimed. "My crew is not made up of foolsss!"

"—and that his crew is looking into it."

"V'hy should they?" Captain Huun't snapped. "V'he do not consider v'heaknessesss in ourselvesss, and v'he certainly don't v'horry about them in othersss."

"Then maybe we shouldn't, either!" Beka snapped back at him.

Rev Bem sighed. "Beka, please. Just because his people might act in such an ethnocentric fashion, that doesn't make it right for us."

"Bem, this isn't the time for a—"

"And morality aside," he continued, "since we do not know

how far the parallels between the two dimensions extend, there's a very real possibility that taking care of one captain means that the other captain will be protected by our doing so as well."

Beka shook her head, knowing when she'd been outmaneuvered. "Metaphysics was never my style, Bem. But what the hell, you've got a good point. We *don't* know all the facts, so we can't afford to not act. But hey, Rommie?"

"Beka?"

"I don't understand the problem. I've seen you do some pretty amazing things. Can't you just, well, synthesize something?"

"I could, but it would still be missing one vital component. And that one component is what I lack."

"And . . . ? If that component can only be found in his home dimension, doesn't that put a damper on the whole thing?"

"The closest analogs," Rommie said after a moment, "can be found in our dimension, and one of those analogs could be altered to fit our need. Assuming, of course, that we had it."

"All right, then," Beka said in resignation. "Since we don't know all the facts, we'd better get that component of an enzyme, keep this captain healthy and hope it means that *our* captain stays healthy as well."

"I v'hould appreciate you not speaking of me as if I v'here not here," the saurian drawled. "Ship, v'here isss the nearest source of thisss mysteriousss component for that equally mysteriousss enzyme?"

Rommie was silent for quite a while, accessing data. At last she said, "I've located a star system that's within relatively easy reach by only a brief Slipstream burst. I can't tell much about it, not at this range, but from what I *can* tell, it does seem to have what we need."

"Wait a minute, Rommie!" Beka protested. "We can't go that far from the anomaly zone. Aren't we going to need to be in this region when the zone reopens? And if we're going to be able to make the switch?"

"That is the most likely way to make the exchange, yes. But if we do not correct the enzyme imbalance within a day, a switch may not be possible, since we may not have a Captain Huun't."

"Bah," he said.

"And we don't know what will happen to Dylan," Rommie continued, "if there is no one in this dimension to be returned to that dimension."

Beka glanced at Captain Huun't, who gave her an utterly inscrutable glance back. He didn't believe he would be sick so swiftly, she guessed—who would?—but he also didn't dare gamble his life on it.

I don't blame you, she thought. *I wouldn't want to be caught in that position, either.*

"We can't do anything until those anomalies reappear," Beka summarized, "we don't dare not have a healthy captain here and now, so . . . let's go find our scaly captain his enzyme."

———

She had herself exactly four hours of free time in which she could actually lie down and get some rest, maybe even get some sleep. So of course, Beka thought, staring up at the ceiling of her darkened cabin, now that she had a chance, no matter how brief, to take a nap, she was wide awake. Wide awake, yes, and starting to worry all over again about which captain was where.

Utter waste of time.

Still grumbling to herself, Beka gave up sleep as a lost job, threw on an easy-fitting top and slacks, and went off to *Andromeda*'s Hydroponics Deck and their makeshift gym. If she couldn't sleep, at least maybe she could burn off all this excess energy and useless worry.

Oh, damn. Someone else had clearly had the same idea.

Not Tyr, Beka thought, *please, not Tyr. I don't really want to argue with him now.*

At first, she wasn't sure who it was. The figure sitting hunched up in a corner could have been just about anyone from Bem to Harper. But then Beka caught a glimpse of green scales. It was the saurian.

Hell, now he'll think I'm stalking him.

Beka started to slip away, but for all her caution, she still must have made some small sound, because the saurian called over his shoulder, "V'hait. I know that you are there."

"Sorry. I didn't mean to disturb you."

"V'hait," he repeated. "You . . . do not disturb me."

He turned to look at her. That saurian face was as unreadable as ever, but his slit-pupiled eyes, alien orange though they were, were deeply shadowed, and the emotion in them was, well, almost human.

The guy's scared! Beka realized with a shock of surprise. *Scared and lonely. Well, what do you know?*

But hey, maybe it wasn't so surprising at that. No matter how strong he might be of mind and body, there were limits to anyone's endurance. Captain Huun't was more alone than any of his race could ever have been before, with no guarantee that he would ever be able to get back.

Moved in spite of herself to something almost approaching pity, Beka sat gingerly down beside him. For an awkward while, there was silence.

Then Huun't said, "Thisss bizarre accident could not have possibly happened at a v'horssse time."

Another silence. Beka broke it in a burst of mixed impatience and sympathy. "Go ahead. Talk. I mean," she added with a wave of her hand that took in the whole ship, "who am I going to tell?"

The saurian gave a soft, wavering hiss that after a startled second Beka realized was his species' version of a rueful little laugh. "An excellent point," he said. "After all, my dimension'sss problemsss mean nothing to thisss dimension. I shall, indeed speak freely." He added wryly, "It v'hill be a relief."

With that, Huun't told Beka the history of a crew, his crew, torn out of their time together with their ship, almost as the *Andromeda* had been, of an empire that they'd rejoined three hundred years later only to find that it had grown stagnant and mired in bureaucracy, and of that one small crew's struggles and determination to make a difference.

When Huun't had finished, Beka let out a soft sigh. "Ah. Well. You may not like this, coming from a 'smooth-skin' and all that, but it looks like we're not all that different after all."

"V'hat . . . ?"

"Our captain and ship made that three-hundred-year jump, too."

"I see . . ."

"Yep. And our captain's also a—" A what? A hopeless idealist? "—an honorable man," Beka decided at last, "working to change things for the better." She paused, eying the saurian, then said in a voice so gentle that it amazed her, "Don't worry, Captain Huun't. We'll get you home."

And get our Dylan back again.

Somehow.

NINE • DIPLOMACY

The name of peace is sweet,
And the thing itself is beneficial.
But there is a great difference
Between peace and servitude.
Peace is freedom in tranquility.
Servitude is the worst of all evils,
To be resisted not only by war,
But even by death.

—CICERO (106 BC–43 BC)

"I sense more shipsss," Rhom'hai warned. "And they are rapidly approaching us."

Hell. Not now, Dylan thought. "Identify them."

"They are not allied to those from before."

"Yes, but you have to have more details than that!"

"They are enemies."

"Oh come on, Rhom'hai. You don't have other data. So how can you be so sure that they're enemies at this range?"

"They are enemies," Rhom'hai insisted.

Oh, great. Here we go again. "All right, then, can you tell us how many of them are out there?"

"There are four shipsss in the new enemy fleet."

"Well, hey," Dylan said dryly, "that's one fewer than before."

"They are approaching usss at their maximum speed, and they are armed with S'reni Cannons. V'heaponsss are fully deployed," she added.

"Ssstolen technology," Bekha said with a snarl.

"Better than unfamiliar technology," Dylan countered. "It gives us more of a fighting chance. Assuming, of course, that we do need to fight. And no," he added before anyone could argue, "fighting is *not* always the only option!"

The mysterious newcomers weren't making the same logistical mistake as the saurian fleet. Instead of forming a wedge, these four ships were nicely spread out, giving them a better chance to encircle or destroy the enemy.

"I take it that these guys are not more ships of your own fleet," Dylan commented.

"No," Bh'em said curtly.

"Any idea who they are, then? No, again? Funny, I don't think that's the entire truth. And no," he added sharply, "I'm not calling anybody a liar!"

Still no answer.

"All right, then, we'll do this my way. Arm weapons," Dylan commanded, "but once again, *do not fire*. I repeat, *do not fire!* Wait for my signal. Bekha, open up a communications channel. See if you can get them to talk to us."

"They v'hon't."

"That wasn't a suggestion, Bekha. That was an order! *Obey it!*"

That last whipcrack of a command, delivered with a force that nearly shook the walls of the Command Deck, actually made the saurian start. Bekha gave a faint hiss—a slight token of angry protest—but obediently began running clawed fingers deftly over the communications panel, hunting a useable frequency.

After a few tense moments, the saurian admitted almost reluctantly, "They're sending us a message."

Well, what do you know? Unlike the mysterious attackers in his dimension, these strangers really *did* want to communicate before attacking. *What a welcome change!* Dylan thought dryly. *And let's hope it's not just more of that blind anger the saurian officer was spouting.*

"On screen," he ordered. "Let's see who we're facing."

"It v'hon't—"

Dylan knew stalling when he saw it. "It will. *On screen!*"

Around him, the saurians had all tensed. Did they, as he'd guessed, already know who they were facing? Or was this just one of those instinctive predatory reactions to the unknown?

But as the image formed on the screen, Dylan . . . just stared, frozen in surprise. So *this* was why Bh'em had been so evasive and Ty'rh so hostile. This was why the saurians had been so uneasy. They knew who they were confronting, all right.

The attackers were human.

So that's it, Dylan thought, staring at the image on the screen. *The slave race turns out to have claws after all.*

Damn it, he was feeling that surge of dizziness again. Something was definitely wrong with him, but now was definitely not the time to analyze himself. He . . . could not . . . give in to it!

Dylan, remembering a technique for fighting space sickness, forced himself to keep sitting absolutely straight-backed, with his head absolutely level, and that did help a little.

These humans, now . . . think.

Unless these humans were suicidal separatists acting on their own—which hardly made any sense—it meant that a good part or maybe the whole human race must have risen in revolt against their saurian overlords.

I can hardly blame them for that.

This little fleet of four ships, though, was too small to do any major damage to the saurian empire. Instead, he assumed, it had been waging guerrilla action in space, picking off saurian ships one by one.

And using stolen saurian weapons against them if what these folks say is true, Dylan added with a reluctant little prickle of admiration.

But why had they powered up their weapons and yet hadn't attacked this ship? Why would they take the risk of opening communications instead?

Now, I wonder . . .

The young man on the other end of the communication was undeniably human. In fact, he reminded Dylan more than a little bit of Harper—always assuming that Harper had been blond and had possessed such fierce dark eyes, and had such a grim, no-nonsense expression. From what Dylan could see of him besides his face, the young man was wearing a somber black tunic that looked like it was part of a quickly designed and makeshift uniform.

Not surprisingly, the young man was staring back at Dylan with equal astonishment. But he had enough presence of mind after that first startled moment to say sternly, "I am S'ian Gerard, captain of *Freedom Fighter Alpha*. Who—and v'hat—are you?"

The Universe, as Bem might have said it, definitely had a sense of humor, a very warped and ironic one. If this had been his rightful dimension, Dylan thought, these folks would probably have been allies whom he would have been busily enlisting. Now, though, he was on the wrong side for that.

He can only think that I'm one of his people, some "smooth-skin" traitor helping the enemy.

You did what you could with what you had. At least the dizziness was once more fading away, hopefully not to return. "As you can see," Dylan said to the other human captain, "I'm obviously not one of these people. But no matter how it looks, I'm not one of yours, either."

"No?" the young man asked sardonically. "Who are you, then?" Sarcasm fairly dripped from his voice. "The Space Angel, perhapsss, or the Spirit of Last Year'sss Sorrowsss?"

"I am Dylan Hunt, Captain of the *Andromeda Ascendant* of another, reasonably parallel, dimension."

"V'hat, isss that the best story that you can concoct?"

"I find it pretty difficult to believe it myself," Dylan agreed. "It just happens to be the truth."

"If this isss some sort of bizarre green-scaled trick, be v'harned: V'he have four ships to your one."

"You know, we've noticed that little matter," Dylan re-torted. "But the fact remains that you haven't opened fire. Why not?"

"V'he are not butchers."

"It's nice to hear that you have a working sense of morality," Dylan said. "But I think that there's more to this than your compassion."

"Perhaps, perhaps not. But that *other* fact remains—there are four of us and only one of you. You, whoever and v'hatever you are, if I were in your place, I would be thinking of surren-der just about now."

Quite predictably, that idea created instant chaos on the saurian Command Deck. The crew sprang to their feet almost as one, all of them hissing savagely and shouting out:

"No surrender!"

"V'he do not yield to smooth-skinsss!"

"They shall not steal our ship!"

"We'll get back to you on that," Dylan said to the human captain over the noise, and signaled to Bekha, *cut channel!*

Bekha actually obeyed him for once, cutting the channel with a vicious stab of claws, and the screen went blank.

Dylan turned to the others, who instantly fell silent, staring at him with hot, angry eyes, all but daring him, the smooth-skin human, to say something of which they wouldn't approve.

"All right, everyone," he began, "I don't know about you, but suicide is not my style." Before they could start shouting again, he added sharply, "Neither is surrender. But I'm telling you here and now to stop acting like a group of bullying children and for once use your heads! And don't interrupt! We have the weapons of four ships aimed at us, damn it, and I am *not* going to die for your pride!"

"You *have* no pride!" Ty'rh shouted.

"Oh, will you just *shut up*?" Dylan shouted back at him. "Either that, or get the hell off this deck!"

As Ty'rh floundered, too stunned by this smooth-skin's sheer gall to do more than sputter, Bekha lunged at Dylan. Dylan hit first and hit hard, landing an uppercut to the jaw, right under the chin, delivered with all his anger.

To his amazed relief, Bekha went down as suddenly as though shot through the head.

What they used to call a glass jaw, Dylan realized, refusing to rub his hand. *Never thought that a saurian would have one.*

"Anyone else?" he asked. "No? All right, then. Someone make sure Bekha gets up again. Bh'em, come with me. We need to get away from these children if we're going to succeed with what I have in mind."

He had a split-second to worry about what would happen if Bh'em refused. But the saurian gave him one quick glance that was plainly full of wary curiosity about what Dylan was planning, and then calmly followed. Dylan led him to the same room in which they'd had their private conversation.

"Bh'em, I'm assuming that you know how to reopen that communications channel?"

"I do."

"And I suspect that you already have some inkling of what I'm about to try to do?"

"Indeed, yesss."

Dylan raised a skeptical eyebrow at that casual acceptance. "I'm not going to commit you to anything you don't want to do."

"I did not think that you v'hould. So. Curiosity isss not always a bad thing. V'he shall sssee."

With that, the saurian reopened the channel.

Sure enough, Captain Gerard was waiting, looking almost too composed for that to be believable.

Not as calm as you'd like to be, eh? Dylan thought. *For what it's worth, neither am I. But all right, here we go.*

"Hello, again," Dylan said to him. "I have some interesting information for you. We know that you folks happen to be rebels against the empire. But what you may not know is that these folks happen to be rebels against the empire as well. Now, isn't that a lovely coincidence?"

"V'hat—"

That came from both the human and the saurian at the same time.

"Wait, both of you, hear me out. Did you ever hear the saying, 'United we stand, divided we fall'?"

"You are proposing an alliance . . . ?" Gerard asked warily.

Ha, yes, that was exactly what he was trying to do in his right dimension, forge alliances. Here, though . . . "Look, I'm not pretending there isn't an issue of mutual prejudice here."

"Prejudiccce!" Bh'em erupted.

"They are the bigotsss!" Captain Gerard shouted.

"Hold on, both of you! There's a time to settle grudges and a time to ignore them for the sake of a common goal. And I feel pretty sure that you both know it!"

He waited half a beat. Silence from them both. Good. They were actually listening.

"Now, I'm not going to claim that you're both acting against the empire for the same reasons," Dylan continued. "I'm neither that naïve nor that arrogant. But you both want the same thing, and what that is, is a change for the better. And hey, I agree with that. I'd say that the wisest thing to do is to win the battle first, and then argue out the details of your goals and prejudices later."

Would they see his point? Dylan pushed boldly forward. "Shall we move on to formal introductions? Bh'em, forgive me if I'm omitting any titles, but this is Captain Gerard. Captain Gerard, this is Bh'em."

He figuratively stepped back to let them make their own introductions, which they accomplished with a minimum of snarling. That they were willing to manage it at all gave Dylan hope. It meant, for one thing, that neither of them was stupid or overwhelmed by pride or bigotry. They both saw the advantages in what he was proposing, and they both knew that those advantages overweighed mutual distrust and prejudice.

He'd had to learn a good many diplomatic skills in his own dimension. Dylan applied them now in full force, overwhelming any opposition with the sheer force of his will.

"You didn't fire on us, Captain Gerard," he said with his most charming smile, "but it wasn't just because you wanted a prize. You were hoping to talk with us. You recognized something about this ship."

"V'he are the *Androom'da*," Bh'em cut in proudly. "All know usss."

"That's right," Dylan agreed. "And we saw proof of that instant recognition when the saurian fleet opened fire on us. While the human ship," he added quickly, "did not. Interesting, isn't it? An axiom from my people states, 'The enemy of my enemy is my friend.'" *And never mind the cynic who said, "The enemy of my enemy is still my enemy!"*

"Hah, that isss true v'hisdom!" Bh'em exclaimed.

"It is," Captain Gerard agreed.

Aha, Step One had been taken. The two sides had actually just agreed on something!

"See what I mean?" Dylan continued. "Now I know that there is a long history of bad feelings between your two species. And yes, before either of you interrupt, I am quite well aware that what I just said is a spectacular understatement. But I meant it to be just that way. For the moment, the present and future are far more important to us all than the past."

"Continue," Bh'em said.

"Think about this: You don't have to like each other, you don't have to try to solve all the issues of the past right now—you just have to be able to make two decisions."

"V'hich are?" Captain Gerard asked, frowning slightly.

"One," Dylan said, "you agree that you can plan together and:

"Two, you agree that you can work together for the same goal."

"Freedom!" the human cried.

"Honor," Bh'em cried.

"Can't have one without the other," Dylan told them, deliberately rushing over the point. "Look, this isn't going to be easy." Never mind the part about overthrowing an empire. That would be easy compared to the fight to overcome ingrained prejudices. "But if you both agree to this," he continued, "you'll have not one and four but a united five-ship fleet between you. And I can't think that you are alone in this rebellion, either of you. Who knows where this alliance will lead?"

Who knows, indeed!

If things start working here, I may have actually just planted the seeds of peace in this dimension. A really weird peace, maybe, not necessarily the most logical or stable, but peace nonetheless.

"Let usss talk," Bh'em said.

It was at that precarious moment that Rhom'hai shouted, "V'harning! The anomaly zone is opening!"

Both ships rocked and shook in the sudden chaos. "Sorry," Dylan said, "can't stay to finish this. You're on your own."

He raced back to the command deck, where he found Bekha, muttering a steady stream of saurian oaths, fighting with the ship's controls. All at once, blazing blue-white light engulfed Dylan. He had time to think, *Not now, not yet, I'm not finished here, I need—*

It didn't matter.

Then there was nothing.

TEN • THE MISSING LINK

In these matters the only certainty is that nothing is certain.

—PLINY THE ELDER
(AD 23–AD 79)

"There it is," Rommie said almost as soon as she'd exited Slipstream. "That is the proper sector, and there is the correct star system, dead ahead. We should be there within one shipboard hour."

She sounded almost smug about the whole thing, assuming, of course, that smugness was possible for her. Or, Beka wondered, could that be relief she was hearing in Rommie's voice? It couldn't have been easy even for Rommie to accurately pinpoint something from so far away.

The star system that Rommie had located quickly grew

larger on her viewscreens as she sped toward it—and it looked less and less appealing with every second.

"Geez, Rommie," Harper said from his usual place in the machine shop that he'd turned into his private laboratory, "you call that a star system?"

"There are four planets orbiting a Class 3A sun. That does, indeed, fit the definition of a star system."

"Oh, sure," Harper countered, "you've got a stable sun and you've got four planets—four utter and complete dust balls. Couldn't you find someplace a little livelier?"

"I was hardly hunting for a system with what you call night life," Rommie retorted.

"Yeah, but this place is dead. I mean, you know, *dead*. Like literally."

"Not quite."

As Harper watched, wondering what Rommie had found, he saw that a space station orbited the fourth planet from the sun.

"Call that a station?" he asked scornfully. "Looks more like an orbiting junkyard."

Beka, on the command deck and overhearing this exchange, silently agreed with Harper. The fourth planet was a barren brown globe like the other three, but one that seemed to have accumulated a partial ring of broken, battered, rusty . . . things. They were, she assumed, the artifacts from who knew how many races. Or maybe that should be their garbage rather than their artifacts.

But an incoming recording, translated by Rommie, quickly

and enthusiastically welcomed them to "The Spacer's Delight: The finest salvage yard facility in the universe!"

"Rommie," Beka asked doubtfully, "are you sure this is the right place? A salvage yard?"

"Yes, it is indeed the right place. In fact, even now I am picking up strong traces of narialum."

"Narialum?" Captain Huun't echoed in surprise. "I recognize that name from my dimension. Isss that not a *rock*?"

"A mineral," Rommie corrected.

"You expect me to eat *rocksss*?"

"Minerals," Rommie repeated patiently. "Ground up, and with their essential atomic structure reversed."

"That part's a piece o'cake," came from Harper. "I could do it in my sleep. Not that I want to spend my sleep working."

"And yes," Rommie finished, "it will work."

"Trust her," Beka said without any expression at all. "Rommie is usually right."

The saurian opened his mouth for what would probably have been some less than complimentary comment. But then he caught Beka's glance and closed his mouth again, presumably remembering their conversation of the night before, and contented himself with merely shrugging.

Beka got busy hunting for and contacting a merchant. He wasn't difficult to find. Actually, he seemed to be the only merchant in the area, according to him the owner and sole proprietor of the salvage yard.

Yeah, right, he's the King of Junk, Beka thought.

His race was . . . well, it was something biped, something

remotely humanoid, with upward pointing ears, huge dark eyes and russet fur all over, but right now, Beka wasn't really interested in species analyses, only in what he—she still assumed that it was he—had to sell.

"My my *my*," he—she still assumed—chirped. "Ship splendid is, yes. Salvage price amazing it would be."

"Our ship is not salvage," Beka said flatly, "nor is she for sale. Is that understood?"

"Sure? Yes? Ah, asking had to do. Is understanding. So, yes, is it as is. And now what need you?"

"Ever hear of narialum?"

"Narialum?" he—she *still* assumed—chirped. "Yes, yes, I got such. Top grade, pure, all that. You want?"

"We could use a little, maybe," Beka drawled. "If it's good quality, of course. It's useful for shining up tools."

"Ha, ha, yes, if you saying this are. Is, you know: Anything saying, as long as paying!"

Just what we needed: a poet. "How much for, say, a double handful?" Beka asked.

"How much you want paying?"

Round in circles. "What do you want?"

"Not knowing what you offering. Ah, yes. Understanding problem am. Language issue, yes? Problem, communicating type, understood. Simple, we solve this as such. Come aboard, me, yes? Talk face to face?"

Beka raised a skeptical eyebrow. "Only you."

"Sure, me, one only. Problem not. Ship always full-fueled, always ready. Shortly be there."

Sure enough, Rommie reported, "A small—no, make that a tiny ship is on its way to me. One life-form aboard."

The merchant clambered out of his tiny ship onto *Andromedas'* hangar deck with not much in the way of grace but what could only be described as a theatrical "ta-da," his furry red arms outflung dramatically. "I am Wurref'Kar, merchant of merchants, owner of the finest salvage yard in all the universe. My, is crowded place, all you here," he added. "And ships, so many!"

"All we here" was Beka, Bem, Tyr and Captain Huun't. How many more might be in the crew (or in this case, weren't) was, Beka thought, none of his business. She didn't much care for that "ships, so many" line, either. That had sounded downright lustful.

Still, Wurref'Kar did look pretty innocuous. He was about the same height and build as Captain Huun't, but covered with that plushy red fur that made him look almost like a stuffed toy.

Looks can be deceiving, Beka reminded herself. But he clearly had no weapons, save for a small sidearm that Rommie quickly scanned and assured everyone wasn't loaded.

"All right," Beka said to the merchant, "before we go any further, let's see that narialum."

It didn't look like much to her: lumps of plain gray rock—mineral, rather, Beka corrected herself. But Rommie said, voice echoing throughout the hanger deck. "It is, indeed, narialum, and of the proper grade."

"Very good," Beka said to the merchant. "Now, we both

know that you didn't make the trip here for nothing. What do you want in exchange?"

"Simple. This ship."

"Very funny."

"Not joke. *Said* it would great salvage price make."

"You're going to take us over all by yourself?" Tyr said scornfully. "What sort of nonsense—"

But Wurref'Kar was suddenly an unbelievable blur of motion. Beka felt a jab on her arm without even knowing he'd gotten that close . . . and suddenly was on the floor, unable to move, realizing only then that she'd been drugged by a long claw on the alien merchant's hand. The others were falling, too, Bem and Trance—whatever drug was in that claw clearly affected many species. Tyr rushed in—but was, for once in his Nietzschean life, caught off guard, because by sheer bad luck, Wurref'Kar happened to be whirling toward him just at that moment, and moving faster than even a Nietzschean could react—

Not faster than Captain Huun't. He had, as a result of Tyr's bad luck, been given that split-second of warning that Tyr hadn't gotten. Wurref'Kar's claw clicked harmlessly against green scales as Huun't lunged at him.

Wow, Beka thought in honest admiration.

Green scales and red fur actually blurred with the speed of their fighting, which was the fastest exchange of blows, blocks, kicks, and yes, clawings by both parties that Beka had ever seen. If she hadn't been stuck flat on her back, half-dazed by whatever drug had hit her, she might even have enjoyed watching it.

Yeah. Right. "See a spectacular display of martial arts as per-
formed by two high-speed experts!"

Now, though, all she could do was think how stupid this
whole thing was, how utterly surreal. And how Captain
Huun't had better win the fight. If he didn't, there would be
nothing to stop Wurref'Kar from simply spacing them all before they could recover.

As if he'd heard her thought, the saurian suddenly dropped,
sending the merchant helplessly hurtling over him, then
twisted, leaped up, and caught Wurref'Kar by the throat.

"Thisss may not be my dimension," Captain Huun't hissed,
"thisss may not be my ship, but damn you, you are not going
to take it! Do." Shake. "You." Shake. "Understand?"

Wurref'Kar snarled—as best he could manage it with that
powerful saurian arm around his throat—but finally muttered
a reluctant, "Yes."

"And v'hat about the drug in your claw?"

"Wear off, will, short while. No harm."

"V'he shall see."

"Letting go?"

"V'he shall see," the saurian repeated.

But sure enough, Beka did feel sensation coming back to
her body, and from the corner of her eye she saw that the others were stirring as well.

"I'm all right," she said, scrambling back up to her feet.

"So am I," Bem added.

"And I," said Trance.

"Of course," a muttered agreement from Tyr.

"Excellent!" Captain Huun't said. "And so you get to live a little longer," he told his captive. "But of coursss you have a fee to pay usss for the trouble you have caused usss."

"Fee . . . ?"

"V'hy, the narialum, of coursss!"

"No!"

"Yesss. Unless, of course, you v'hish to pay your life to usss as v'hell."

Wurref'Kar sagged. "Take the narialum."

It wasn't until the dejected merchant had left, and Rommie was well on her way back toward the anomaly zone that Captain Huun't said, "I . . . feel suddenly most unv'hell . . .", and collapsed.

"I *said* that he required that enzyme," Rommie said.

Much later, back on the command deck and back in the region of the anomaly zone—or rather, where the anomaly zone should be—Beka asked the now-recovered saurian, "Why?"

He was clearly a much happier individual after that restorative dose of the missing enzyme. "V'hy v'hat?"

"Why did you fight for us?"

"V'hat, did you think that I v'hanted to be stranded so far from the anomaly zone?"

"There's more to it than that."

"Eck. So there isss."

"And . . . ?"

"And I am a captain, this isss, if not my ship, at least the parallel of my ship, and you—you showed me a side to smooth-skinsss—to humansss, rather, I v'hill say, that I had not known."

"I'll take that as a compliment," Beka said dryly. "And I have to say that I am rather—"

But she never got to finish that. Rommie suddenly cut in with:

"The anomaly zone has reappeared! Warning: The anomaly zone has reappeared!"

"Captain Huun't! Watch out!"

She couldn't see him, just that blue-white light, and Rommie was saying, "Captain Huun't is not on board."

But suddenly someone was there. The figure that was now standing in an aura of bluish light was not saurian. He was human.

"Dylan . . . ?" Beka wondered.

No. The man did look superficially like Dylan, with the same build, the same hair color, even if he was in a uniform of rather gaudy blue and red that seemed more than a little out of place aboard a ship. But Dylan had never looked so . . . elegant, so perfectly groomed. Or so utterly out of his element.

"Oh hell," Beka said. "Here we go again. I only hope Captain Huun't did make it home."

"I beg your pardon?"

"Never mind." She forced a smile, feeling like the attendant on some in-system shuttle flight. "Welcome to the *Andromeda Ascendant*, the best ship in your new dimension."

ELEVEN • OF POETS AND PACIFISTS

Those who fail to learn history
Are doomed to repeat it;
Those who fail to learn history *correctly*—
Why, they are simply doomed.
—ACHEM DRO'HM,
"THE ILLUSION OF HISTORICAL FACT," CY 4761

For a stunned moment, Dylan was sure that he must have died. He didn't actually remember dying, or even suffering any sort of injury. And surely those bouts of dizziness couldn't have been fatal. But here he was, lying on something that was wonderfully soft, softer than his bed on *Andromeda Ascendant*, and there was a lovely fragrance all about him.

And now that he'd opened his eyes, this soft pink place didn't look like any part of *Andromeda Ascendant*. For that matter, this soft pink place didn't look like anything from any ship he'd ever been on, including the saurian version he had just, ah, left. *Was* he . . . dead . . . ?

But then reality and a clearer mind set in together. He was still very much alive, and it was the saurian-inflicted scratches across his chest, covered with some medication, that smelled faintly floral. And no heaven could possibly be this, well, pink. The walls were pink. The ceiling was pink. The sheet covering him was pink. And even the dress of the blonde young woman bending over him was pink—

Whoa, wait a moment. Never mind her outfit. If her face was a little less soft, if her eyes were a little less, ah, vapid . . .

"Beka?" he asked in disbelief.

"You're awake!" she cried with obvious delight. "I was beginning to worry a little bit about when you would wake, and if you would be all right when you did wake. I guess you are! All right, I mean. But I'm afraid that you have my name a little wrong: it's Becci. And you aren't—you don't really look like—well, you do, but you're not, not really, are you?"

"Ah . . . what?"

"Oh, sorry. When we passed through all that—that strangeness, that anomaly zone, when that weird light hit us, whatever it was, you-he-our captain vanished. Then he—no, you, you reappeared, all scratched up and, ah, very much out of uniform. And you collapsed right there on the deck."

Oh, hell. Wrong dimension again. This time I must have been dumped with too much force for my mind to catch up with the change.

"When our doctors studied you," Becci continued, "we found that you were lacking a trace element. That problem would have been making you feel ill—it was, wasn't it?—and they said it might even have eventually killed you if the lack continued. But don't worry; they corrected it while you were unconscious. You're perfectly healthy again."

That, at least, explained the dizziness he'd started to feel while he was aboard the saurian ship. It probably explained his blacking out just now, too. Well, at least that was one less thing to worry him.

"I know this is a cliché," Dylan said, "but, ah, where am I?"

"Why, you are aboard what is the finest ship in any fleet, of course: the *Andi Dromda*."

"The Andi . . . Dromda," he repeated carefully.

Thinking of strong, determined Rommie as anything as cute as Andi—no. *Better than Rhom'hai, though*, Dylan thought. *Easier to pronounce.*

Uh-huh, and this was Becci, not Beka. And all this prettiness—this was definitely not related at all to the saurian dimension. Or to his own.

Lord. Does that mean that I'm getting farther away from my dimension with every jump? Or isn't there any logical pattern to this dimension shifting at all? Will I have to go through every possible dimension to get back to the starting point? Or won't I get that far at all?

"That's right," Becci continued eagerly, unaware of Dylan's uneasy thoughts, "and *Andi* is, as I've said the finest ship in the entire fleet of fine ships, and—Oh, wait, no, you shouldn't get up yet, not before the doctors say that you can, no, wait—oh. Oh my."

She turned away quickly, but not so quickly that Dylan

couldn't see her blushing a bright red as he got to his feet. And in that startled moment, he realized why: Someone must have stripped him of that battered pair of saurian slacks, and not bothered to replace them. With anything. He was stark naked.

O . . . kay, at least the crew had left him clothing, including a rather stylish suit of some silky, royal blue fabric. It fit almost unnervingly well, and belted with a scarlet sash. Red boots completed the outfit.

Feeling more like a fashion plate than a captain, Dylan told himself, *Hey, at least it isn't pink!* "You can turn around now."

"Oh. Oh! Now you really do look a lot like him. Our captain, that is."

"And that would be . . . ?"

"Why, Captain Hund, of course, Daylan Hund."

Well, at least there weren't any glottal stops to trip up his tongue this time. "My name is Captain Dylan Hunt," he said, annunciating carefully.

Her eyes widened. "That's amazingly close, isn't it? My, you really are from another dimension, aren't you?"

Okay, these folks had apparently already figured that out without any help from him. Score one for their side. "Yes, I am," Dylan said. "Now, take me to the Command Deck. Please."

What did happen to the saurians and the human rebels?

Dylan found himself really wanting to believe that he'd played a part, no matter how small, in the overthrowing of a tyranny and that he'd helped in the birth of a new interstellar peace. Or that at the very least that he'd helped to plant a few of the seeds of peace.

I'll probably never know the answer. For that matter, I'll probably never know what happened to the saurian Captain Hunt, either. I wonder, did my saurian alternate make it home, or is he still stuck like me, doing this ridiculous dimension-wandering routine?

Damn, never mind that, I just wish I knew what was happening aboard Andromeda. My Andromeda, *that is.*

That type of thinking was going to drive him crazy. Shaking his head at the insanity of the universe or universes or whatever, Dylan followed Becci out into the ship's corridors.

It was . . . it was like walking into a really strange art gallery, a long, narrow tube of one. All available space on the corridor walls was covered with murals painted in soothing shades of pink, purple, green, and blue, curving up across the ceiling, which was painted to mimic a clear blue sky. Dylan saw landscapes of Earth and other worlds, starscapes and swirling, colorful nebulas, and even a few gentle abstracts worked in soft pastels—

What is *this place?*

"Here we are," Becci said brightly.

Dylan winced. The Command Deck was almost as . . . well, as pretty as he'd feared. After the jarring ugliness of the saurian ship, this place was overwhelmingly slanted on the other side of the esthetic scale. It seemed designed to enfold him in a gentle blending of blues, grays, and pastel purples. Delicate painted traceries of leafy vines twined their way across every flat surface, occasionally bursting into sprays of white flowers. Individual computer consoles rose like elegant blue and purple blossoms on curving green stalks from various command stations.

Good God, Dylan thought. *I've fallen into an arts festival.*

The people didn't look like anyone he knew, or even wanted to know. Neat and elegant in their blue uniforms, they looked more like images of idealized officers than the real thing. Each of them, he realized, wore a sash in a different color, yellow, green, orange, presumably indicating rank.

"Captain!" a young man exclaimed eagerly, then stopped in confusion.

He might as well get this over with as quickly as possible.

"No, I'm not your captain. I am Captain Dylan Hunt of the *Andromeda Ascendant* from an alternate dimension. Your captain is probably in my place aboard my ship right now. And yes, I do want to get back, and yes, I'm sure your captain does as well."

"Oh, we knew about all that already," a dark-skinned, gentle-faced man said with a wave of his hand. "We are already working on the calculations to get him back—and you as well."

Something about the lines of that gentle face—good Lord, no, this couldn't be . . . "Tyr . . . ?" Dylan asked warily.

"No, sir, I'm afraid that isn't my name. I am Terri."

Fighting down the impulse to say, *Aw, no, you're not, you're playing a Nietzscheans joke on me even though Nietzscheans don't joke,* Dylan simply dipped his head to the man in courtesy and received a gracious bow in return.

"Well, since you say you're already working on the calculations," Dylan said, "have you any clues yet about how you're going to get your captain and me exchanged yet?"

"Unfortunately, no. We have nothing yet." That came from a fresh-faced youngster. "But don't worry, sir. We are still working on it."

Dylan blinked. "Harper?"

"Why yes, I am a harpist!" the youngster said with an eager smile. "I'm Harri. But how did you know?"

"Uh, never mind."

Terri. Harri. Becci. Andi. All right then, it was a cultural thing; names in this dimension ended in "I." He could live with that, even if it did make this all sound abominably, well, cute.

"Sir? If you wish to sit in the command chair, we won't mind."

He gladly sat. Art festival? This was more like some wandering interstellar art colony! "Who else is on board?"

The next to be introduced was a young woman called Traci—a version of Trance, Dylan assumed—who announced in a no-nonsense voice over the comm channel that she had just run a new diagnostic and was working on others.

Okay then, in this dimension, she must have taken over Harper's place. He could live with that.

No Bem, though?

"No," Becci told him, frowning slightly at Dylan's description. "There are no aliens aboard this ship. And there is certainly not anyone so—so ugly on board this ship, either."

"Hey, hey, the Rev's not ugly. Not below the surface, any-way. He's one of the gentlest and most kindly souls I know."

"Of . . . course he is." She was clearly humoring him.

Great. They're beauty bigots.

Okay, it's not my issue. And let's keep moving right along, Dylan told himself dryly. He asked, "How many are on board?"

"We have a full crew aboard right now of 4,132 men and women."

"Four thousand one hundred and thirty-two . . ." he echoed weakly, a little prickle of what was almost wonder stabbing through him. That had been the original number of Rommie's full crew. In this dimension, then, he . . . they . . . hadn't been lost in time.

They're not my people, he reminded himself sternly. *No one I'd know. This is an alternate dimension. Remember that.*

"But how did you all get here?" Dylan asked. "I mean, what sent you all three hundred years into the future?"

They stared at him as though he'd announced that space had just turned a pretty pink.

"This *is* our time," Becci said very gently.

"But . . ."

"Ah, I see the confusion. It may not be so in your dimension, but here it is Andi alone who is three hundred years old."

"I, uh, see."

With a faint shimmer, the ship's avatar appeared. It was Rommie, Dylan realized with a start—that was if Rommie had decided to look like a slim, pretty, smooth-faced girl of perhaps eighteen, her slight form clad in flowing, diaphanous blue veils.

"Three hundred years *young*," she corrected sweetly. It was Rommie's voice, all right, but pitched almost an octave higher and with an almost syrupy quality. "Ooh, and who are *you*? You're *pretty*!"

To his embarrassment, Dylan felt his face grow warm. But before he could find anything safe to say, Becci gave an exaggerated sigh, shaking her head in mocking reproach.

"Andi!" she scolded. "Stop teasing the poor man. You know perfectly well who he is."

The girlish face pouted. "No one ever lets me have any fun." Her image shimmered dramatically and vanished.

"Interesting," Dylan managed to get out.

"You'll have to ignore her," Becci said with a smile. "She's been like that ever since she accessed those silly romance tapes."

"Huh," the ship said. "The ones that *you* brought on board."

Dylan, desperate for a touch of sanity, looked about the room. "But I don't really understand. What are you, all of you, doing out here?"

"Exploring!" Becci exclaimed.

"Looking for new forms of art," Terri added.

"New types of music," Harri the harper continued.

Lord. This really is *an art colony.*

"Then . . . there's no trouble back home?" Dylan prodded gingerly. "Back on Earth, I mean."

Becci frowned slightly. "Why, no. There's nothing out of the ordinary. Everything is nice and quiet."

"You've never heard of the Nietzscheans?"

The others exchanged puzzled glances.

"In the histories, of course," Terri began uncertainly.

"I know!" Andi cut in, this time not bothering to materialize. "It was back when I was first commissioned. The Nietzscheans were a sect of foolish humans. They followed the beliefs of a sour person who hated everyone." (*That did sum up Friedrich Nietzsche pretty well*, Dylan thought.) "And they tried to build themselves into a super race and cause problems for everyone else. But their attempts to take over everyone and everything failed, and they were taught the error of their ways."

"That was three hundred years ago, then," Dylan said, trying to make his way through the verbiage and pin some facts down.

"That's right."

"Ancient history," Harri added.

"And there have been no other problems since then," Becci finished with a charming smile. "We have been at peace since then."

Floundering, Dylan asked, "But what about outside trouble? Trouble from alien races?"

This time there was the faintest of pauses before anyone answered him. He had, Dylan thought, clearly just gone beyond their boundaries of good taste. Didn't they like aliens? Or was that, rather, didn't they like anyone they believed not to be as attractive as themselves?

"We haven't had any trouble," Becci said firmly, and in her

sweet voice was the faintest hint of a warning. "Our ancestors might have been a war-making sort, to their shame, but we are not."

Or was that the problem here? Did talk of weapons or warriors equal bad taste to them?

"I do still carry weapons," Andi added. "Fully functional, too, because I refuse to have anything dusty on me! But I have not needed to fire any for several human lifetimes."

"We do not fight," Terri said firmly.

They can't be that innocent. Dylan thought.

Or maybe they can at that. Three hundred years of absolute peace—if there really can be such a thing when humans are involved—probably could breed whole generations of pacifists.

But this dimension can't be that peaceful. I won't believe that. It can't be that different from my own or I wouldn't have made the transfer in one piece.

Maybe these folks have just all been amazingly lucky so far.

"You, uh, don't fight at all?" Dylan asked, testing. "Even when it becomes necessary?"

Becci shook her head with a slight, condescending smile. "No offense meant, Captain Hunt, but I'm afraid you just don't understand."

"Try me."

"We're all Gandhians aboard this ship, or at least most of us are."

Gandhians . . . ? From the name Gandhi? There'd been several politicians bearing that name in the past centuries. "Are you," Dylan guessed wildly, "referring to Mahatma Gandhi?"

"Very good, sir! Of course we are."

Oh. "But that Gandhi lived back in the, ah, the twentieth century."

"That's quite right, sir. No one alive, obviously, has ever met him, but his teachings are still being studied. The Gandhian movement began over two hundred years ago. It is based, of course, on that great man's teachings."

Passive resistance. Might work against other humans, but I'd like to see someone try that move on the Magog. "Well, I'd agree that peace is one of the top ten goals of the universe, or should be, but surely not every species respects or understands passive resistance."

"There is no issue that could be settled by fighting that can't be better solved by peaceful means."

"Well, that is the ideal situation, but—"

Seeing them all starting to frown at him, Dylan cut himself off. He had to live on this ship for . . . however long, and one didn't make waves with one's hosts. "Never mind. I'm still a little bit dazed."

Not exactly a lie, and not surprising, either. He had gone from a warrior crew to a pacifist crew of artists aboard an alternate Rommie who also seemed to have pacifist leanings.

And my folks back in my dimension now have a pacifist captain who has suddenly been thrust into the middle of a definitely nonpacifist crew, and our definitely violent universe.

I only hope that everyone survives.

TWELVE · CURIOUSER AND CURIOUSER

If you don't know where you're going, any road will
take you there.

—LEWIS CARROLL

This elegantly clad, perfectly groomed figure definitely wasn't
the right Dylan. Dylan was rarely actually unkempt, but even
at his best, he had never looked quite so . . . flawless.

The man, whatever alternate Dylan he happened to be, took
one dazed look about the Command Deck. His glance stopped
short at Bem, he stared at Bem for a moment, and then he said
weakly, "Impossible."

With that one word, the man's eyes rolled up in his head,
and down he went in a limp heap.

"Fainted," Tyr said scornfully.

Beka waited one more moment to see if the anomaly zone

was finished delivering alternate Dylans and might this time by some wild chance actually deliver the right Dylan.

No. No more arrivals. The ship lurched violently, and Rommie warned, "We cannot stay here much longer."

"You got it," Beka said, and grabbed the ship's controls. "Hang on, everyone. We're out of here."

It meant piloting *Andromeda* back out of what felt suddenly like an interstellar slalom course, forced to swerve left, right, left again, struggling to stay at a safe distance from those damned randomly opening mini-wormholes.

As she fought to keep them moving and safe, Beka dimly was aware that Bem, being Bem, was already kneeling at the fallen man's side to tend him. She heard him say, "Yes, he has fainted, nothing more. The sudden shock of transfer to here from his dimension must have simply overwhelmed his mind."

No kidding, Beka thought. *It's been overwhelming mine, and I'm not even changing dimensions!*

Speaking of which: *Hope that Huun't got back home. He was a pretty decent guy after all.*

And where oh where is Dylan, our Dylan, now?

This time, no one was really surprised when Rommie announced, "The anomaly zone has just vanished again."

"Okay, folks," Harper said from his lair, "I've got it pretty much pinned down by now. The anomaly zone is a really weird rift in time and space, I'd say mostly in space but partly in time as well, and it's allowing people, or at least a person, to slip from dimension to dimension. I haven't been able to get enough accurate figures to be sure of its exact size and power. And right, there's this, too: We don't know for sure how many dimensions are involved in this rift—"

"Over a thousand," Trance said softly. "That could support life we'd recognize, that is."

Beka didn't even raise an eyebrow. You didn't ask Trance how she knew what she knew. You just accepted that she knew it, and moved on from there.

"Okay," Harper said after a second. "Make that a *lot* of dimensions. And we don't know why the damned thing seems to have zeroed in only on Dylan Hunt and Dylan Hunt variations—something to do with his specific pattern of molecular frequencies, maybe—but at least we do know that much."

"Harper," Beka began.

"I'm working on it, I'm working on it."

Tyr snorted. "He sounds like a child with a new toy."

"That's our Harper," Beka said, fighting against a sudden lurch of the ship. "Always after something new." *Sure, it's fun for him, he's not doing the piloting. Or that jumping around from dimension to dimension.*

Trance had joined Bem, kneeling beside him at the man's side. "He's awakening," she murmured.

The man stared up at her in what seemed like genuine wonder. "I don't know what you are," he said in a voice that was full of delight, "but you are a truly lovely creation."

Then he caught sight of Bem kneeling beside her and recoiled in shock, scrambling to his feet. "Who—what—"

A lot of people did have that reaction to him, Beka thought. *After all, waking up to find a Magog looking down at you, especially at such close range, wasn't exactly a pleasant way to greet the day.*

People didn't, however, generally add after that first shock, "What is this ugliness doing on this ship?"

"Hey, hey," Beka said, "watch your words. This is Rev Bem, an honored member of our crew!"

The man turned sharply at her words to study her, and then frowned slightly. "You . . . almost look like Becci."

"And you . . . almost look like Dylan, but you sure as hell aren't him. Who are you?"

"Why, I am Captain Daylan Hund!" he said in a tone that told her she should recognize him.

"Not on this ship, you're not," she retorted. "The captain on this ship is Dylan Hunt." She pronounced it carefully.

"Ah. You . . . said something . . . just before I passed out. Another dimension . . ." He rubbed a hand over his eyes. "*This* is another dimension."

"Yes."

"And he, your captain, whatever his name, are you trying to tell me that he's in my place on my ship?"

"That about sums it up, yes."

He ran a hand through his shining, perfectly groomed hair. "This is . . . this is amazing."

"It is, isn't it?" Beka agreed dryly.

"And this ship, this really is an alternate of my *Andi Droomda*. Amazing. But it's so . . ."

"Similar? Familiar?"

"So plain!" Captain Hund exploded. "Do you not have any artists on board?"

"Ah, not really."

"Musicians?"

"No."

"Poets? Composers? No? No one like that?"

"Sorry, no."

"Good heavens," Captain Hund said, "just what manner of benighted ship *is* this?"

"I am not benighted," Rommie said, suddenly appearing before him in her most kick-butt leather-clad persona. "That concept applies to humanity, not AIs. A ship cannot, by definition, be benighted."

The alternate Dylan stared. "Andi . . . ?"

"No. I am *Andromeda Ascendant*. Rommie to my crew."

Well, he *was* an alternate Dylan, and like their rightful Dylan, was clearly able to think on his feet.

"I seem to have gotten off to a bad start," he said with a gracious bow that somehow managed to include everyone. "Please, mark my bad manners up to the shock of my sudden arrival." Captain Hund gestured at the command chair. "If I may?"

Beka shrugged. "You're the captain just now."

He sat with a heaviness that told Beka the man might be a little less in control of himself than he was pretending. Hey, maybe he really was feeling the shock of all this change after all.

Well, yes, of course he was, she scolded herself. Whatever else he was, Captain Hund was only human. He would be made of far sterner stuff than most mortals if he didn't feel stunned.

All right, then, she'd give Captain Hund the benefit of the doubt. Beka started over, more formally introducing herself and the others, including the absent but always vocal Seamus Harper, who gave a casual "Yo!" from his "lair" in the machine shop when his name was called.

Captain Hund flinched all over again at the sight of Bem, although he did raise his brows again at the realization that this being was a monk and as such, to be honored, not rejected. But this time, wisely and probably politically, he said nothing.

When Beka had finished her introductions, Captain Hund frowned slightly and asked, "But what about the others?"

"The . . . others?" This time it was Beka's turn to frown. "I don't understand. We're it."

"But—what—so few? On a ship this size, so few?" Captain Hund stared at her, at them all, in what seemed like genuine horror. "Dear Lord. What disasters struck you?"

"Wait a minute. Are you trying to say that your ship—"

"Has a full crew, yes, of course. There are over four thousand of us on board, as there should be."

"Oh," was all Beka could say. "I, uh, see." She took a deep, steadying breath. "Captain Hund, I really think that we need to talk. There's a lot more to this situation than you think."

Captain Hund sat back in his chair, staring at Beka. ". . . and so your Captain Dylan Hunt is from three hundred years in the past," he continued.

"That's right."

"So is your ship."

"Yes."

"But the rest of you are not. You are from this time."

"You got it."

The man shook his head in wonder. "Amazing, absolutely amazing. I must say that it all barely sounds possible to me."

Beka gave a sharp little bark of a laugh. "To me, too."

"And in this dimension the Nietzscheans are still real, still active, and not merely characters in the history books."

"Alive and well and a real pain in the . . . well, you get the picture."

"Unbelievable."

"Yeah, that does pretty much sum it up. But don't worry too much, Captain Hund, you probably won't be stuck here with us bothersome, artless sorts forever. The anomaly zone does seem to be determined to keep switching Dylans on us, so the odds are pretty good that you'll get back home. Eventually."

"And you'll get your captain back again." His sudden smile was so charming and so utterly *Dylan* that Beka's heart gave a lurch.

"Yes, well, in the meantime," she said, "we need a captain, and it looks like you're it."

"So I am." He leaned forward in sudden enthusiasm. "Now, we both agree that there's not much that we can do constructively except wait for the anomaly zone to make up its mind to reopen, so . . ."

"Yes?" Beka prodded warily, not sure where he was going with this.

"So, I thought perhaps we could start doing something about fixing up the décor in this place!"

"I'm going to kill him," Beka said to Bem as they walked down one of *Andromeda*'s corridors together. "I am going to kill Captain 'I'm So Charming a Pacifist' Daylan Hund."

"Surely not."

"Want to bet? I mean, come *on*! I don't care how self-controlled and kind-hearted you are, Rev, even you have limits. So far our charming Captain Hund has managed to insult you ever time he looks at you—when he does deign to look at you at all."

"That is his sad weakness," Bem replied gently. "Believe me, Beka, I'm used to such a reaction from humankind, and it would take a great deal more than one man's reaction to make me forget myself. Such shallow sight is his issue, just as he can only follow his own path, and hopefully learn along the way to see more honestly."

"That's nice," Beka said dryly. "I'm glad to hear that you have such a charitable view of things, and I wish that I could share your view. But it still doesn't change the fact that I am going to kill him."

"Ah."

"Did you hear what he said to me? Did you? Never mind that I just saved his bacon, everyone's bacon, by getting *An-*

dromeda clear of the anomaly zone. No, what he said to me was just that I would be much prettier in pink. Prettier! Damn it, Bem, this isn't a fashion cruise!"

She broke off, glaring at him suspiciously. "You're laughing at me."

"No. I am laughing at the entire ridiculous situation. Here we are trapped in a place of chaos that is calm for the moment but just might rip our poor Rommie apart without warning, waiting for Dylan, our Dylan, who may or may not arrive, and all the while that we wait here away from everything, we are using up food, water, and air supplies that we can't leave here to replenish."

Beka stared at him, wondering if a Magog who was also a Wayist monk could suddenly go over the edge. He'd just named all the things that had secretly been worrying her, and he was *laughing* about them?

"Well, golly gee, Rev Bem," she drawled, "that there scenario you've just described sure does sound funny."

"No," he said quietly, "it isn't funny. Nor did I intend it to be. Ah, but let me explain myself with some wisdom from your homeworld. 'I laugh, that I may not weep.'"

"Ah. Got it."

Just then, Rommie's voice, sounding downright aggravated for her, announced, "Will someone please convince this alternate captain that no, I do *not* wish my corridors ornamented with pretty floral scenes?"

Beka sighed. "Hold that thought, Rev. I have to go rescue Rommie from a paint worse than death."

But by the time she arrived at the coordinates that Rommie had given her, Captain Hund was already gone. *I guess he couldn't find the right color paint,* Beka thought dryly.

Where had he gotten, though? Back, she hoped, to the Command Deck like a nice, sensible captain.

No. At least the Rev's voice from the Command Deck told her that Bem had gone back there, so *someone* was keeping watch on things. But if Hund didn't turn up pretty soon, Beka was going to have to take his place on the Command Deck, and to hell with any down time.

"I *am* going to kill him," she muttered. "Rommie? Where has our wandering captain gone now?"

"The Hydroponics Deck," Rommie answered promptly. "I believe that he's currently having a discussion with Trance about . . . flowers."

"I can believe it," Beka said, and headed off that way.

But when Beka got there, she found only Trance, who was looking, even for Trance, downright dazed. "Captain Hund isn't here any more," she told Beka. "He just stopped by here to look things over, and then he told me that I should be growing prettier flowers. More pink ones especially."

Beka shook her head. "He does seem to have a thing about pink. And if he's on a self-imposed fact-finding mission, inspecting everything on board, we may not see our wanderer for some time."

"Aren't you worried that he'll get into trouble?"

"Don't tempt me," Beka said shortly, and headed on back over to the Command Deck.

Where she found, surprise, surprise, that Captain Daylan Hund had already returned.

"Well, hello!" he said from the command chair, giving her his very charming smile. "I was wondering where you were."

Looking for you, you idiot! Where do you think I was?

No. She couldn't say that. With great restraint, Beka contented herself with saying instead, "Captain Hund, I really wish that you would let someone know before you go off wandering about this ship."

"Why, certainly I can't be in any danger here!" he retorted, his eyebrows raised in what looked like genuine surprise. "This is simply an alternate version of my own ship, after all. Aside from the, ah, let's call it the unfortunate lack of artistic merit, its layout is not all that strange to me. And if my presence should suddenly be needed," he added with a cheerful grin, "well now, certainly your lovely Rommie could instantly notify me wherever I happened to be aboard the ship of any problems that required my immediate attention."

At first Beka was sure that the man was simply being sarcastic. No one could possibly be so naïve.

But then it hit her that yes, maybe he *could* be that naïve at that. Three hundred years of utter peace . . . no threats, no dangers, no challenges . . . nothing to alarm or stimulate or in any way really test the human psyche . . . three hundred years of complete pacifism . . .

Oh, great. Now the whole thing, all his easy, silly actions, his apparently total lack of common sense, all of it became perfectly clear. They had themselves a pacifist captain here in a most unpacifistic universe. And, Beka thought, they could only hope that nothing drastic or violent happened between now and whenever they exchanged Dylans.

"Captain Hund," Beka began, "I know that you come from what sounds like a truly wonderful dimension, an utterly peaceful one. But believe me, this dimension is very different from the one you know. This dimension has fangs. It bites. Do you understand me, Captain Hund?"

He leaned forward. "I understand that you are worried about me. I find that very touching, my dear—"

"Touching!" Beka exploded. "Damn it, man, I'm not trying to protect you, I'm not some pretty little girl in pink, I am just trying to keep you alive long enough for us to get our own Dylan back again!"

"Of course you are."

"And don't patronize me!"

"Good heavens, of course not! I wouldn't dream of it."

"Of course not," Beka echoed dryly.

Dylan, wherever you may be, how in God's name are you dealing with an entire crew of pink-loving, flower-loving, art-loving, peace-loving . . . no way out of the convoluted thought but—pacifists?

THIRTEEN • WAR AND PEACE

Let him who desires peace prepare for war.
—FLAVIUS VEGETIUS RENATUS,
DE REI MILITARI

Wasn't this all just *wonderful?*

And yes, Dylan told himself wryly, if anyone could have heard his thought, that was definitely meant as sarcasm.

He shook his head, still not really believing the situation. This time the dimension switch had dumped him aboard an *Andromeda*-analogue that had a full crew, yes—but a full crew of poets, musicians, and artists—oh yes, and with maybe a token working scientist or two, a few medics and some mechanics—and with not a single military person among them.

Well, maybe the lack of any trained fighters wouldn't matter this time. Maybe his stay in this dimension would actually be as incredibly peaceful as it had seemed so far, and he would actually be able to relax a little—as much as all this prettiness would allow—and enjoy an enforced vacation, so to speak. Maybe he'd be able to be patient and just wait for the next inter-dimensional transition to come along and transport him home like . . . heh . . . like a kid coming home from art summer camp.

Why can't I believe that?

"You know," Dylan began conversationally to the others on the Command Deck, since at the moment he couldn't think of anything more useful to say, "the one person I haven't met so far who seems to be a parallel of someone on my own ship is Trance—ah, Traci."

"Oh, you don't want to meet *her*," Becci said dismissively.

"Why not?"

"She's a little . . . odd."

"So's the Trance in my dimension. 'Odd' doesn't bother me."

"You don't understand, sir. She likes to play with those messy, smelly machines."

"It's a rough job," Dylan said dryly, "but someone's got to do it."

"I suppose." That had a sulky tone to it.

Now isn't this nice. Gandhists or not, they're still good old human beings. And it looks like we have here a good old-fashioned female rivalry on board. I can just hear Beka on the subject now!

He wisely decided to let the subject drop. If Becci didn't see the irony of a pacifist holding a grudge against another pacifist, he wasn't going to be the one to point it out to her.

Time passed.

More time passed.

After still more time had passed, nothing much had happened on the ship. It began to look as though nothing much would. Getting to his feet and stretching, Dylan excused himself.

"I'm going to take some time off and stretch my muscles. No," he added with a fake smile, "you don't have to accompany me. This is a parallel of my own ship, after all, and I'll certainly be able to find my way around it by myself without getting into any trouble, ha, ha."

Did I actually just say, "Ha, ha?" Lord, I've got to get out of this place before it really *starts getting to me!*

It took a great deal of Dylan's inner fortitude as he went through the ship's corridors to get used to the idea of there being a full crew aboard *Andromeda*—all right, then, aboard *an* Andromeda. All of the crewmembers whom he met were dressed in their stylish, silky uniforms, all of them perfectly neat, perfectly tailored, and perfectly groomed. It was, he thought, like one big, never-ending fashion show. He'd forgotten just how crowded a fully crewed ship could be.

And all of the crew members smiled peacefully at him and happily greeted him as though it were the most ordinary thing in the universe to meet a parallel captain from another dimension.

Those uniforms were, as Dylan soon realized, color-coded: Blue for officers, red for techs, green for medics, and yellow for what he mentally dubbed miscellaneous workers. The colored sashes did, as he had already suspected, represent different rankings within the general divisions. His blue uniform and bright red sash was worn by only one person: the captain.

A very bemused one.

I need to be alone, Dylan decided. *Really alone, that is. I need to give myself a chance to judge things on my own. And all this cheerfulness is really starting to annoy me.*

Dylan finally did manage to elude everyone—no, he corrected that to not quite everyone. While trying to avoid a group of sweetly smiling young crewmen and women, he nearly tripped over a small pair of feet. Ah, he must have just accidentally located the mysterious Traci, who was hunkered over by an opened instrument panel, half hidden inside the space within.

At first, though, he wasn't at all sure this was she. Oh yes, the person he'd found was as slim and graceful as the Trance he remembered, but she was wearing coveralls covered with grime and grease, was very fair-skinned, with the faintest hint of lavender to her, and had sleek but definite muscling he certainly didn't recall seeing on the Trance in his dimension.

"Hey, Captain," she said cheerfully, peering up at him out of the narrow opening, "what are you doing in—no, wait, you're still the other one. The other-dimensional captain, I mean."

"That's right. I'm Captain Dylan Hunt of the *Andromeda Ascendant*."

The young woman wriggled a little farther out of the

cramped space so that she could squirm around and get a better look at him. "Well, I'm sorry not to have been on the Command Deck with the others to greet you when you made that really unexpected arrival, but, here, look at this: You can see that this whole board needed replacement pretty quickly."

"Isn't that, well, the job of the mechanics?"

"Normally, yes, but hey, with so big a ship, they can use my help. Besides," she added with a gamine grin that definitely reminded him of his Trance, "I'm good with my hands."

He just nodded helplessly, watching her deftly connect cables and recalibrate panels. "See?" she said, still cheerfully. "The ship speaks to me through my hands, and I answer her as best I can."

Kneeling beside her, Dylan watched, beginning to grow fascinated in spite of himself by her quick, elegant work.

I met Beka the Fullback on the saurian ship. Now here's Trance the Mechanic. What's next? Harper the Supermodel?

What was next was the voice that said over his shoulder in indignant tones, "Captain! What are you doing here?"

He turned to see Becci looking down at him in downright disgust. "I beg your pardon?" Dylan asked in surprise.

"This is hardly the place for you, sir. You have higher status than this, even as an alternate to our rightful captain."

Dylan got back to his feet. "I thought that Gandhi was against things like caste systems."

"Sir, this has nothing to do with that."

"Doesn't it? Becci, this is a legitimate part of the ship, and

Tranc—ah, Traci, Traci here is doing a perfectly fine job. There's no shame in that, or in any honest work. And I don't see why a captain shouldn't be free to investigate all the aspects of his own ship."

"Sir, I don't mean to argue with you, but I really must remind you that this is not actually *your* ship. And I'm sure that you agree with me when I say that it can't be right for you to damage the reputation of our own captain when he returns."

That didn't make a bit of sense to Dylan, but he chalked it up to a little more of intership jealousy. That well-known phenomenon—in which minor rivalries and arguments could easily grow up into outright warfare over nothing much—did happen when you took over four thousand people and kept them in a closed environment for any decent length of time. Dylan had almost forgotten about that little quirk of human psychology, what with the small size of *Andromeda Ascendant*'s currently far less than crowded crew.

Not that our little group of happy star wanderers always gets along so well at that!

"Very well," Dylan said formally. "I will continue my tour.

"Alone," he added, when Becci would have followed him. "Please understand: I certainly am quite well aware that this isn't actually my ship. But it is a parallel of my own. And as acting captain, I have the responsibility of making my own, unbiased inspections."

Which was as close as Dylan could politically get to what he really wanted to say to her, which was something along the lines of *Leave me alone, you silly little bigoted creature*, without being rude.

It worked. Becci stalked away as though he had actually told her she was a fool, with a barely audible "Humph."

With an inner shrug, since he hardly cared what she thought of him, Dylan continued his tour.

Hey, what was this . . . ? Music? Yes, it was, and coming from the Hydroponics Deck.

What a charming sound!

The musician was a young man . . . ah, yes, it was Harri. Off duty now, he was perched on the rim of one tank of what looked like red-leafed lettuce, playing softly on a small harp. The melody was so gentle and sweet that at first Dylan stood transfixed with the unexpected pleasure of it.

But after a short while, the enjoyment faded. Dylan realized that the melody was also awfully repetitive, consisting basically of the same few phrases repeated over and over again. It quickly became downright boring, in fact.

Well, why should I be surprised? It's just as pretty as everything else, and just as empty.

Dylan started to leave as quietly as he could since there wasn't any reason to disturb Harri and his music. But the young man looked up just then, saw him and called out, "Ah, Captain Hunt! I see you're hunting for a bit of tranquility." He laughed. "Did you get that? It was a play of words on 'Hunt' and 'hunting.'"

"Couldn't miss it."

Harri was still grinning at his own cleverness. "Won't you join me for a moment, sir?"

Dylan could hardly refuse. "For a moment," he agreed politely.

He stood listening to a little more of the pretty, vapid harp music. And then, figuring that he'd been polite long enough and didn't need to hear any more of it, Dylan started to move on. But Harri glanced up at him and then murmured over his harp, "Don't trust him."

Dylan stopped short, frowning. "Him? Him *who*?"

"Terri. Sir, I know this sounds petty and all that, and beneath the serenity of a Gandhian, but, well, I have to warn you just in case. Don't turn your back on him. And above all, don't believe the things that he says."

Dylan's frown deepened. "Why not?"

"Well . . ."

"Come on, Harri, you can't say such things and not explain them in greater detail. Are there any solid reasons behind this warning?"

"Oh, well . . . no, there's nothing specific, sir."

"Then why—"

"Not yet, at any rate. But he just . . . well . . . they say . . ." Harri's voice dropped to a conspiratorial whisper. "You may have noticed this. He's the only darker-skinned man on this ship. They say that that's because his great-great-grandparents were *Nietzscheans*!"

"No!" Dylan gasped in pseudo-horror. "Imagine that!"

"It's true." Harri waved a finger at him. "Be careful!"

"I always am. Thank you," Dylan said solemnly and walked on.

Lord. What a nasty little creature that is. Harri the harpist is as bad as bigoted Becci.

Suddenly soured on the subject of exploration, Dylan headed back toward the Command Deck. Sure enough, with perfect ironic timing, the next person he came upon was Terri, the great-whatever possible descendant of Nietzscheans.

"Captain?" he murmured to Dylan. "Please listen. I'm afraid that I have a warning for you."

Of course you do. "About Harri?" Dylan hazarded.

"No! Certainly not!" That sounded like genuine surprise on Terri's part. "No, sir, I'm talking about Becci."

"What about her?"

"Well . . . nothing that I can put a finger on."

"Then don't say anything."

"But I need to warn you. You, ah, you just can't trust her, Captain Hunt. That's all that I can tell you right now. Just don't believe anything she says."

"I'll take it under consideration," Dylan said curtly, and stalked away, silently fuming.

What childishness! What utter, useless, perilous childishness! With no outside tensions or alarms, the crew had started in sniping at each other.

Maybe Captain Hund didn't care about the problem, or maybe he didn't even notice it. Who knows? Maybe he was even a part of it.

But if I have to be stuck here on his ship, I am not going to put up with being the focus for all their pettiness.

"Everyone," Dylan said over a ship-wide communications link. "This is Captain Dylan Hunt speaking. I am calling an emergency meeting right here and right now. Officers, get up here on the Command Deck on the double. Everyone else, stay by an open link. That is an order!"

Soon after that, confronted by a circle of puzzled faces and with that ship-wide communications channel open as well and knowing that everyone was listening to him, Dylan opened fire.

"What sorts of idiots are there on this ship?" he began. "Are you adults or children? And no, damn it," he added as Terri opened his mouth, "those were *not* rhetorical questions!

"You call yourselves Gandhians. All right, don't bristle at me. I have no quarrel with that, and believe me, I'm not making fun of anyone's beliefs. I wouldn't be that rude or that stupid.

"I just want to know how much about Gandhi and his teachings you actually know. Aside from the idealized ideas, that is. Mahatma Gandhi and his followers had a reason for what they did. They had a government they were resisting, a genuine challenge they were struggling to overcome. They were trying to liberate their country. And while they worked to free India," he continued, "they did *not* waste their time hunting for enemies within their own group!

"You, though—you have no enemies outside this ship.

You've already been very careful to tell me that. You have no real enemies—and so, instead of realizing how fortunate you are, you're inventing your own enemies from within your own crewmembers just for the hell of it! Because you're bored! Accusing each other of lying, of gossiping, of being of the wrong ethnic or political backgrounds—I received three vague and unproven warnings within the last hour alone. Funny, though, how when I asked for details, for proof, there were none!"

"But . . ." Harri began.

"*Silence!*" Dylan shouted. "Have you ever really stopped and listened to yourselves? For that matter, do you ever stop and just think? No, of course you don't! You have nothing to challenge your brains but painting pretty pictures and making pretty music!

"And as for those stupid claims you've been making, do any of you have even the slightest proof that any of them are real? Well? Do you?"

He waited for a few tense moments, watching those on the Command Deck squirm, and then continued, "Bah. I thought not.

"All right, then, everyone, listen to me! This is an order, not a suggestion, an order:

"This childish behavior stops here and now! Anyone who is caught whispering gossip to anyone else, anyone who is found passing rumors or threats—anyone who is caught doing anything to damage anyone else or anyone else's reputation without just cause is going to spend the rest of this mission in the brig! This is a ship, not a playground! *Is that understood?*"

There were some reluctant, "Yes, sirs."

Good enough. "Dismissed!" Dylan shouted.

Most of them went, murmuring angrily to each other. He caught surreptitious hostile glances from those, like Becci and Terri, who needed to stay here on the Command Deck.

Well, Dylan thought wryly, he'd accomplished two goals just now. He had solved the gossiping and sniping problem. He'd also united the crew. They all now had a new enemy in common: him.

Too bad, he thought. *If they don't shape up, they aren't going to survive the first challenge that finally does come their way.*

For what seemed a very long time, nothing at all happened. There was utter silence on the Command Deck.

And then Andi announced with a suddenness that made everyone jump, "Foreign ship approaching."

And here comes the challenge now, Dylan thought.

"On screen," he ordered.

He saw, and instantly, with a coldness settling in the pit of his stomach, recognized what he was seeing.

Oh. Hell. Just what we don't need.

That was definitely and undeniably a ship of the Magog.

The Magog of this dimension, at any rate. Maybe, just maybe this version wasn't quite as bad . . . ?

Who am I trying to fool?

But there appeared to be at least one thing about them that was very different from the Magog in his dimension, because Andi said suddenly, "Captain Hunt, they wish to communicate with us."

The Magog had a language? More to the point, they understood a language used by humans? Whoa, there was something
new! At least in Dylan's dimension, they never really communicated with anyone outside their own species—and in fact, it was
doubtful if they really communicated much at all.

Of course, they could speak quite clearly in a human language if they wished to do so. Rev Bem was a case in point.

But Bem was one of a kind. The average Magog didn't seem
to see the need for much in the way of speech of any sort, at
least not when swarming as a horde hunting food and hosts for
their eggs, which was the only way that most non-Magog got
to see them.

"Go ahead," Dylan said warily.

The image came up, wavered disconcertingly, and then sta-
bilized . . .

Dylan froze at the sight of the horrifying face on the screen,
but not because of its ugliness or the fury contorting it and
blazing from its eyes.

"Good Lord. Bem!"

"It knows this one!" the Magog snarled in surprise, but not
the slightest hint of any recognition flickered in its hot, hungry eyes. "It cannot be. This one does not know it."

"But your name *is* Bem!"

"Name? Is not. That is useless thing. We hunger, that is all!
This is warning to you."

The communication was abruptly broken.

Great, Dylan thought, just great. Maybe the Magog's name
wasn't Bem in this dimension. But it was still he. Which meant

that in this dimension, the good Rev had not become a Wayist, or else had taken what he wanted from that faith, such as human speech, and had then rejected it.

In this dimension the Rev Bem had, instead, impossible though it seemed, become a Magog warlord.

FOURTEEN · MUTINY

> When pacifism is confronted by the Magog, pacifism is
> faced with a problem with which it cannot cope.
> The conventional pacifist conception of a fair and
> reasonable peace is absolutely irrelevant to this reality.
> —AMBASSADOR ERNST WEICK,
>   "ON THE PROBLEMS OF INTERSTELLAR MORALITY,"
>   CV 4781

"What . . . is . . . *that*?" Becci asked, her voice quavering.

"That," Dylan said shortly, "is a Magog."

"He's so—so *ugly!*"

"And so hungry," Dylan retorted. The ship-wide channel
was still open, and he announced to the entire crew, "Listen to
me, all of you, we don't have any time to waste in arguing:

"The Magog are enemies of everyone but other Magog—
and I'm not even so sure about that part. They're predators,
and they're damned good at it. Passive resistance or any other
Gandhian techniques you may happen to know aren't going to
mean a thing to the Magog except that they won't have to

work so hard to catch their prey. They are always hungry, and what they eat is anyone or anything they can catch. The Magog have poison in their fangs, razor-sharp claws that can shred anything short of metal, and oh yes, they are asexual and reproduce by laying eggs in a living host, which is then eaten alive by the young as they hatch."

He looked about at the Command Deck crew, seeing the same fixed, horrified stares on them all. "Never mind the stares. We have to take action, and we have to take it now!"

"We, uh, maybe we could parlay?" Terri asked.

"Forget that!" Dylan snapped. "What you just heard that one Magog say was the most talking that any Magog's ever done!"

"Can you be sure?" Harri wondered.

"Yes, damn it, I can! You can't parlay with them, you can't reason with them, you can only fight or run!"

"Then we should run!"

"More than one ship is out there now," Andi commented. "There are three in all, and they could cut us off if we tried to flee."

"Do you see?" Dylan all but shouted. "There is no other choice. *We have got to fight!*"

"No!"

"We are Gandhians!"

"We never fight!"

"Fighting is never the answer!"

"It is this time!" Dylan exploded. "If you want to live, you have to defend yourselves!"

"Impossible!"

"We will not hurt another living creature."

"Not just hurt," Dylan retorted. "Will you please wake up and face the facts? This isn't a game! This isn't a test of your moral beliefs! If you are going to survive this, you are going to have to kill!"

"Oh no . . ."

"Not that . . ."

"Our captain would never want fighting!"

"He would never ever condone killing!"

"Not like you!"

Dylan sensed rather than saw people moving about him and turned in sudden alarm—just in time to meet a rush of bodies. They weren't just those of the Command Deck crew. Other members of the crew must have stolen in here while he'd been arguing with the officers. It was open mutiny—if one could call it mutiny if it was aimed against a captain from an alternate dimension.

"No, you idiots, you can't—"

They could. As they rushed him, Dylan fought back with unabashed ferocity. Damned if he was going to wind up as the prey of even an alternate-dimensional Magog horde. And damned if these fools were going to send him there! He kicked and punched and even bit, sending one after another of the earnest pacifists flying since they had no idea how to fight back, let alone to fight dirty.

But more and more of them kept rushing him, crowding onto the Command Deck, backing Dylan step by step against a console. And at last the frantic crew overpowered him by sheer numbers. They dragged Dylan to the command chair and bound him there with their sashes despite the fiercest of his struggles.

"You utter idiots!" he shouted.

"You are a disgusting warmonger!" Becci shouted back at him. "We are peacemakers!"

Harri added fiercely, "You've been preaching violence at us all ever since you came aboard."

The others all agreed, their voices overlapping each other in their panicked frenzy:

"Our captain would never—"

"—be so dangerous—"

"—vicious—"

"Gandhianism is the way—"

"—not killing, never killing!"

"Give peace a chance!"

They almost deserved what was going to happen to them, Dylan thought, after that last cliché.

And then, to his utter horror, he saw and heard the crew open up a new communications channel with the Magog. "Pray forgive our captain's rough language and behavior," Becci began. "He is not our real captain at any rate, merely an unfortunate temporary substitute."

Terri continued, "We are a peaceful people. We don't wish to fight with you. There's no need for that. Instead, we simply wish to parlay with you. Surely we can talk everything out."

It was, predictably, the alternate Bem who answered. He

seemed to be the spokesperson—or perhaps the only speaking Magog—on their ship. "Is good." His smile was downright terrifying in its fanged glory. "We send over small scout ship of . . . diplomats."

"No!" Dylan shouted. "You damned fools! You're inviting your own deaths to come and get you! Listen to me, curse you! Accept that I *know* the Magog! You can't reason with them, you can't talk peace with them—you can only fight them! What they want isn't peace, it's your lives!"

No one paid him the slightest bit of attention.

"Listen to me!" he insisted frantically. "You haven't got a chance against the Magog!"

Becci did turn to him at that. "Oh, please. Beings who are as truly ugly as those are certainly our inferiors."

She followed the others out with her nose in the air like an indignant socialite, and Dylan was left alone on the Command Deck.

Astonished, furious, and downright frantic, he at once started working on the sashes. The fabric was tough as silk, curse it . . . yes, but these guys weren't used to anything as, well, as violent as tying someone up. They didn't know how to do the job right—fortunately for him.

But they'd made up for their lack of skill in the sheer number of knots that they'd tied. Swearing under his breath, Dylan began untying the blasted knots one by one, his fingers frustratingly clumsy with the need for haste. Damn it, damn it, this was taking too long!

"A craft is landing on the Hangar Deck," Andi announced over the ship's communications system.

"No!" Dylan shouted, looking up from his struggle. "Andi, no! Close the hanger doors! Close them now!"

"I can't do that," she answered sweetly. "That would mean overriding the crew's request."

"Damn it, Andi, this is the captain speaking! My order overrides all others! Close the doors!"

Another few knots untied.

"I'm afraid that it is too late for that request, Captain Hunt. The craft has already landed on the Hangar Deck."

Damnation! "Give me a visual! Andi, let me see what's happening on the Hangar Deck!"

Nothing. The screen remained dark.

"Andi!"

Nothing.

Still more knots untied.

"Andi! Give me that visual!"

"Trouble!" Andi erupted. "Oh no, oh no, oh no!"

With one last frantic squirm, Dylan was free. "Andi—"

"Trouble! Trouble! Trouble!"

"Andi! Hangar Deck on screen!"

"Oh no, oh no!"

Could a ship's AI go hysterical? No doubt about it: This one apparently could and had. Dylan raced to a console to do the job himself, but—curse it, the controls had all been altered, presumably to make them look more "artistic," and had pretty floral designs covering their proper functions. He couldn't immediately figure out what was what.

"That is an order!" Dylan shouted, still hunting for the right control, trying not to hit anything dangerous, and not sure whether or not the ship would actually listen to him. "Andi, come on, listen to me! This is Captain Hunt! You are to put Hangar Deck on screen *now!*"

There was a final gasp of "Trouble." And then, as if worn out by the strain of her own hysterics, she obeyed.

Until that moment, Dylan had been hoping that somehow, amazingly, impossibly, he would be proven wrong, all his fears groundless, the Magog in this dimension not like those he knew but a kinder, gentler lot.

But the horror that was suddenly revealed onscreen was totally as terrible as he'd expected.

Dylan, teeth clenched, watched the Magog horde sweep over the defenseless pacifists with the relentless fury of a tidal wave. He watched men and women go down screaming under the assault of claws and fangs, their blood spewing over the Magog and splattering the hanger floor and walls. The terrified crew struggled with each other in their mindless frenzy, fighting to retreat back into the body of the ship, punching and shoving each other aside, climbing over each other, trampling the fallen. And all the while, the Magog swarmed after them.

We can't let the Magog get into the whole ship! Dylan thought in horror. *Good God, there are over four thousand helpless lives at stake, pacifists who have never even held a weapon—it would be a Magog orgy of food and death—*

How could the pacifists possibly defend themselves against the Magog? With paintbrushes and harps?

Damn it, damn it, he was the only one with military training! He had to do something!

I can't let so many innocent people die!

But what could one man possibly do? Dylan had a sudden ridiculous image of himself rushing blindly in, guns blazing—assuming, of course, that he actually *had* guns—wiping out an entire Magog horde all by himself, like one of those impossibly heroic captains out of the children's stories—

No, no, stop that nonsense, think of something practical, something that can actually be—

And then Dylan froze, feeling a cold weight of horror settle within him. Oh yes. There actually *was* a way to stop the Magog. Yes, and like it or not, it was the only possible way.

It's going to mean the deaths of some innocent people.

Yes, but the hard, cold truth was this: It came down to either sacrificing a few, or losing everyone on board.

It had to be done.

That didn't mean, Dylan thought grimly, that he was going to enjoy it.

FIFTEEN • A THING THAT MUST BE DONE

The Art of War?
Never mind what all those books say.
There are only four rules.
One: Locate your enemy.
Two: Attack him.
Three: Hit him as hard as you can.
Four: Get the hell out of there.

—ADMIRAL ARDEN SMITH, RETIRED,
CV 4198

Every captain, Dylan thought grimly, eventually came up against decisions that he had to make, no matter the cost or how much they hurt.

"Andi," Dylan commanded flatly, "seal off the Hangar Deck."

"But some crew members are still—"

"Do it!"

Teeth clenched, he watched her seal the Hangar Deck shut. Yes, it had worked. The Magog had been caught off-guard in their frenzy, trapped in there, at least for the moment.

But so had some of the crew been trapped—injured maybe, dying, maybe, but still alive.

I have to do this. There are over four thousand innocent lives at stake.

"Open hangar outer doors," Dylan commanded.

"But—"

"That is an order!"

Dylan watched without blinking, refusing to allow himself to think too deeply about what was happening at his command. The sudden depressurization of the deck as the hangar doors opened to the vacuum of space pulled both Magog and humans helplessly out of the ship, pinwheeling on to their deaths in the endless emptiness of space.

Still refusing to think about what he'd just done, Dylan snapped, "Andi! Check for any life forms remaining in the Hangar Deck. Include any within ships or other enclosures."

"There are no life forms within the Hangar Deck." Andi's voice sounded stunned, utterly devoid of emotion.

"What about the corridors from the Hangar Deck? Find and identify any foreign life forms there!"

"There are three invaders in Corridor A."

"Damn!" No use expecting the untrained pacifists to be able to fight off three furious, desperate Magog. "Andi! I need a weapon, any kind, anything you can find that works. Now!"

What she found for him was a sidearm of some archaic sort that he'd never seen before. No matter. It was recognizable as a gun, it was powered up, it had a clearly identifiable triggering mechanism, and it could be used. Dylan fought his way through mobs of terrified crewmen and women, shoving and even punching them aside without stopping, leaping over the fallen, keeping going against the flood of frantic humanity until he'd reached Corridor A.

Yes! He suddenly had a clear shot at one of the Magog. But one of the frantic crew jostled his arm, and the shot went wide, scorching the ceiling instead and fortunately not blasting a hole in it. The Magog charged him, going right over fallen human bodies, its fierce gaze fixed on his face, but Dylan managed to get off a wildly lucky second shot that took off its head.

It fell straight forward. The blood-spouting body blocked the other two Magog for an instant. That instant was just long enough for Dylan to fire again. He hit one of the Magog but didn't bring the creature down. The other Magog clawed its way over its dead comrade, heading toward Dylan. But to Dylan's astonishment, the crew turned on it before he could fire, attacking it with the wild savagery of people suddenly driven beyond the bonds of sanity. Hitting and slapping it, they couldn't bring the Magog down—but they did delay it long enough for Dylan to shoot it at pretty near to pointblank range.

Two down.

The third Magog, the one that he had already wounded, was busy bringing down every crew member within its reach, biting, clawing, struggling with all its terrible strength to get to Dylan, who by now it knew had the only gun. The Magog lunged, swiping at him, and its outstretched claws hit the weapon with such force that the gun went flying from Dylan's hand.

Ow! Damn!

But suddenly it didn't matter whether or not he recovered the weapon. The crew was still caught up in its savage mob frenzy, and this time there were enough of them together to pull the wounded Magog right off its feet. From there on, it became a massacre—but of the Magog. Dylan drew back in shock at the sight of what a horde of maddened humans could do to what had just been a living being a few moments ago. Lord, when they sobered up and realized what they'd just done . . .

But he couldn't waste time here. The internal threat was gone, but those Magog ships were still out there. Dylan ran back to the Command Deck at top speed, hurling himself breathlessly into his chair.

"Andi!" Struggling not to pant, Dylan commanded, "Locate all the Magog ships. Show them onscreen. And activate your weapons."

"I . . ."

"Do it!"

"I can't . . ."

"Andi! You said that your weapons were in working shape."

"They are, but . . ."

"This is no time for Gandhian behavior! You want to have a human crew or a Magog invasion?"

"Human." It was a whisper.

"Then obey my order, curse it! Show the ships onscreen and activate your weapons!"

The screen instantly lit up. "Weapons activated," Andi said in a suddenly flat, completely mechanical tone.

I must have just overridden something in her system, this time hopefully for good, or at least until the danger's past. Her crew can get her cute self back later—if they still want it.

Dylan rushed to what he thought should be the weapons console, assuming that its position matched the one on his *Andromeda*. He hesitated only a moment at the sight of the flowery vines painted all over it. Then, determinedly ignoring all that ridiculous prettiness, he stabbed his hand down blindly for what memory told him should be the right buttons.

Ha, yes! That much, at least, was still the same as on his *Andromeda*. The console lit up just the way it should, announcing to him that he was now in manual control of all the ship's weaponry.

The Magog ships . . . there were three of them. A smaller fleet than he'd feared, but three to one odds weren't exactly his favorite.

One Magog vessel was facing this ship while the other two were circling about, keeping one on either side of him. Not an ideal situation for him, but space was, after all, three-dimensional, and three ships couldn't completely box him in. But could he manage all this, piloting, maneuvering, and firing, single-handedly?

Wouldn't be easy. But then, when facing the Magog, what was? Still, it would be nice to have *some* help, and quickly!

Just then, a figure staggered onto the Control Deck, stumbling and nearly falling—

"Becci!"

She was bloodstained and bedraggled, her blonde hair a tangled mess and her pretty uniform nearly in shreds, but her eyes were clear and utterly cold. She said flatly, "We must kill them. All of them."

"Well, yes, this time I fully agree with you. And believe me, you couldn't have picked a better time to show up. Take your place at navigation and be ready to move at my command."

The first Magog ship, the one that was captained by the Bem-analog war leader, was already powering up weapons. Dylan didn't wait to ask this dimension's Bem what he intended to do. No doubt about those intentions at all: If you can't eat it or lay eggs in it, destroy it. Particularly since the Magog must have just seen some of their comrades spaced.

Foolish of you guys to risk your leader. Tough.

Dylan's first shot hit the Magog ship just to the right of the bow, doing less damage than he would have liked. But the force of the impact skewed the ship about to broadside. Dylan hurriedly got off a second shot, fired before the Magog could react, and hit truly amidships. The Magog ship suddenly and dramatically exploded into a red-orange-white fireball.

Oh Lord, I hope that I didn't just kill off our *Bem in our dimension as well!*

Hell of a time to think about that possibility. Particularly since he couldn't do anything about it now.

"Good," Becci said, still in that deadly cold voice.

But for all the coldness, she had the self-control to send them sweeping away from the expanding force of the explosion.

The remaining Magog ships were recovering their positions, too, and had weapons online.

"Left, ten o'clock!" Dylan ordered, hoping she understood since he had no time for more detailed coordinates.

Becci got the point anyhow and sent the ship hurtling at a sharp angle from where they'd been. A blast of energy shook them violently, but Andi hastily assured them, "No damage."

There was the second ship, turning to meet them, weapons ready. Dylan was ready, too. And . . . fire! The shot missed the body of the Magog ship, which was already in motion, but caught it across one engine, sending it spiraling away before it could get off a shot.

Dylan didn't wait to see if the Magog were space-wise enough to get themselves under control. They were out of the battle for the moment at least, and that was good enough. He ordered Becci, "Right, two o'clock!"

The third Magog ship was already turning, already opening fire—this time they weren't going to escape unscathed. "Brace for impact!" Dylan shouted over the open link.

The sudden rough impact threw the ship violently about in space, nearly hurling Dylan and Becci from their chairs. But Becci was grimly clinging to the console.

"You don't get away," she muttered, sounding almost like Beka. "You don't get away from me. Not so easily."

"Damage report!" Dylan demanded.

"Deck Five, Section Two," Andi reported. "No life forms were within it when it was struck. There is minor decompression damage."

"Seal off Deck Five, Section Two," Dylan ordered. Repairs could wait. He turned his attention back to the third ship. Its captain or the hive mind or whatever was controlling it was bringing it back around for another sortie. "Oh no, you don't! Becci—"

"I see it."

She brought the ship into a twisting roll that took them safely past the Magog ship. Dylan saw his chance and fired, raking the underside of the Magog ship—yes! He'd torn it open. Now the Magog would have to retreat, seal off the damage and limp away—

No, they wouldn't. Either they didn't know how, or they'd reacted too slowly. There was a localized explosion, then a larger one—

As Becci held their ship steady against the shockwave from the final explosion in the series, Andi commented, rather needlessly under the circumstances, "Two ships are now destroyed."

"Give me the condition of the remaining ship," Dylan commanded.

"The second ship, the ship whose engine we hit, has now lost all power. It cannot fight and hangs helpless in space."

Oh hell, Dylan thought. It had been bad enough to space Magog and humans in order to save this ship. But to destroy a defenseless ship such as this one would be committing cold-blooded murder. And even if it was a shipload of Magog . . . *I can't do this.*

"Kill them," Becci said coldly.

"Becci. Didn't you hear what Rommie said? They can't defend themselves. They can't hurt us."

"Kill them!" Without warning, Becci leaped up from her chair and brought her fist down on the weapons console, nearly smashing Dylan's hand in the process and hitting the launch button squarely.

The single blast of fire from that attack hit the defenseless Magog ship squarely and took it out in a rolling series of explosions.

Dylan sat back with a sigh, watching as it slowly struck Becci what she had just done, watching as the prettiness faded from her face and the horror turned her eyes to blue ice.

Innocence lost. Forever.

"Come on," he said gently. "Becci, come on. Time to weep later. The others need our help."

Moving like a sleepwalker, she followed him off the Command Deck—into a world of chaos. The other crewmembers certainly did need help. The medics, themselves looking as dazed and lost as the rest since they, too, had never seen real violence, had their hands full with the number of injured, dying, and stunned. Many of those crew members who seemed physically unhurt were just aimlessly milling about in complete and utter shock.

Ha, there was Terri. He looked a little less dazed than the

rest and a little more responsible. Dylan caught him by the shoulders.

"Terri. Terri! Come on, man, listen to me. Focus. We need someone on the Command Deck. Can you handle it? Terri? Can you handle it?"

The confused gaze suddenly sharpened. Face grim, Terri said, "Yes."

"Good man."

Dylan gave him a slap on the back to get him moving, then turned his attention to helping with the nasty task of mopping up the corridor where humans and Magog had died, since few of the crew seemed able to deal with that.

Not that I like this, either. But at least I've seen violent death and its aftermath before. These people . . . I wonder how many of them are going to survive the shock to their minds and bodies. I have a horrible feeling that the medics are going to be kept busy for a long time by a sudden rise in attempted suicides. If they don't try that route themselves. It isn't easy, seeing your entire world and belief system crash down around you.

At last the corridor was cleared of its horrible burden. The Hangar Deck still remained to be cleaned, but there was a limit, Dylan thought, to what even he, with his experience with the real, violent, universe, could endure. That could wait. Instead, he headed back to the Command Deck to relieve Terri.

But things weren't to be so simple. The crew followed him, one blank-eyed mob crowding the corridor. They were, Dylan

thought, overdosed on horror, with their innocence lost and
nothing yet to replace it. They said nothing, but they clearly
blamed him, the stranger, the outsider, for all that had happened.

And Dylan could think of nothing to say that would get
through to them. He took a wary step back, thinking that his
only hope was to get to the Command Deck, barricade it,
and hope that the anomaly zone reopened before someone
thought to cut life support to there.

Yes, but he wasn't going to make it. The mob was just too
close, and getting closer. Of course Dylan knew he could take
down some of them with his bare hands, trained as a fighter as
he was, but he didn't want to harm people whose only crime
was . . . naïveté.

However, he also didn't want them killing him. And even if
he did take some of them down, that wasn't going to stop a
mob. Dylan suddenly thought of that Magog, shredded into
unrecognizable bits by people who'd never before even raised
a hand in violence.

Just then, the ship shook violently, and then seemed to
eerily quiver. Another Magog attack—

No! Dylan recognized this: The anomaly zone was doing its
sudden reappearance!

Sure enough, Andi announced to them all, "Warning. The
anomaly zone is open. Warning. The anomaly zone is open. I
must be piloted away from here."

The mob seemed only to understand one thing: that their
prey was about to escape them. They rushed him, hands out-

stretched to grab him and pull him down the way they'd pulled down that Magog—

Just then, Dylan sudden felt himself engulfed by the now-familiar blue-white light—

And even as the mob clawed at him, he was suddenly—

Not there.

SIXTEEN • CHOOSING A NEW PATH

Here's everything I know about war:
Somebody wins, somebody loses, and nothing is ever
the same again.

—ADMIRAL CONSTANZA STARK,
HIGH GUARD CHIEF OF STAFF,
CY 9784

Beka was busily carrying out a silent argument with herself.

Should she simply once again go mentally through what was rapidly becoming her mantra of choice, *I'm going to kill him?* Or should she, this time, just once, actually go through with the threat? It would be justified. Captain Hund had once again gotten off a dig at her not being, as he put it, pretty in pink, and it would be oh-so satisfying to squeeze his neck till his face became pretty in pink—

But at that moment, perhaps fortunately for them both, Rommie announced, "There is a ship in the vicinity."

"Only one?" Captain Hund asked.

"Precisely."

"Can it have been caught in the anomaly zone as well?"

Gosh, gee, you clever man, you think so? Beka thought, but contented herself with saying dryly, "All things considered, it really couldn't have come from anywhere else."

But then she leaned forward in sudden alarm, studying the image of the ship. "Rommie . . . is that . . . ?"

"Yes. It is, indeed, a Magog ship." She added, "No other ships of that species or any other are anywhere in the vicinity."

"Status," Beka said.

After a few tense moments, Rommie reported, "It does not pose an immediate threat to us. The Magog ship has been badly damaged, presumably by its transit through the anomaly zone. Power aboard it is down to approximately ten percent of what should be the norm for such a vessel. Life Support is also just as low."

"Life-forms?" Captain Hund asked sharply. "What about that?"

"It is difficult to be certain. Some of the Magog may still be alive, but many of the others are surely dead, while still others may already be so close to dead that they do not register on my scanners as living beings."

"Can any of the ship still support life?

"Yes," Rommie said after a moment. "It does seem likely that at least some of the corridors can still support life at minimal functions. This means that at least some of the crew is almost certainly still alive but that most are unconscious. The damage would have occurred too swiftly for most of them to don protective suits. Assuming," she added, "that the Magog actually do carry suits."

Hund glanced earnestly about at the others. "What's the matter with all of you? Why aren't you reacting? That's a ship in trouble."

"Yes," Bem said without inflexion.

"We can't just sit here! We must help them."

"Oh, I don't think so!" Beka retorted. "You may not know who or what they are, Captain Hund, but those are Magog in that ship!" At his blank stare, she summarized quickly, "They're predators, complete, absolute, merciless predators. There's no softness, no arts, no sweetness or redeeming social value to them at all. Got that? The Magog would kill and eat us as soon as look at us—oh, except, of course, for the few captives they'd keep to serve as living hosts for their young to feed off and eat their way out of."

Hund winced at her words, but continued gamely, "Even so, even so. We can't just let them die!"

"Sure we can."

"Oh come now! Morality aside, there's the law. I don't know how it stands in this dimension, but in mine, Interstellar Law Number 105 Subhead A states clearly that 'no disabled ship shall be left unaided so long as there are life-forms aboard in need of that aid.' "

"Yeah, we probably have a regulation like that, too, though I can't rattle off the number and subhead. I'll just say that there are exceptions to every rule."

"Not to this one."

"Wanna bet?"

"No, indeed, there is not," Bem said softly.

Beka turned to him sharply in surprise. "What are you saying? That we should help . . ." She trailed off awkwardly, belatedly remembering that the good Rev, too, was a Magog.

"I admit to being truly torn about this," he continued. "Those aboard that ship are likely to be my people in genome only. But as a true Wayist, I cannot allow any living things to suffer. Whatever they may have done or not have done, those Magog should not be abandoned to die a slow death on a dying ship."

"Simple solution," Beka said. "Blow 'em out of space. Quick, merciful, and final."

"You can't mean that!" Captain Hund cried in horror. "I will not be a party to cold-blooded murder."

Rommie announced just then, "I have finished my survey. There are, indeed, still living beings aboard the Magog ship, but no one is conscious."

"I repeat," Beka said, "Blow 'em out of space. They're already out of it. They'll never feel a thing."

"We will *not commit murder*!" Captain Hund all but shouted.

"Who said anything about murder? Never heard of a mercy killing?"

"A killing is a killing!"

"Hey, guys!" Harper shouted over the communications link. "Don't want to interrupt the interesting ethics debate, but

think about this. We got us a perfect chance to scout out a Magog ship without any hassles. See what makes their ships tick.
Maybe even see if they've got any new technology."

He sounded, Beka thought wryly, almost as if he was licking
his lips about that possibility.

"That gives us *two* reasons to be humane," Captain Hund
said, "and one of them is perfectly practical." He got to his
feet, glancing around at the others. "As acting captain, I
hereby authorize a scouting mission. And just to show that I
don't merely talk morality, I shall lead it."

Beka sighed. "Count me in." At his startled look, she
shrugged. "Someone's got to keep you in one piece. Anyone
else? Tyr?"

"In."

"Me, too!" Harper yelped.

"Sorry, Harper," Beka said. "Got to leave you here." Before
he could start to argue, she added, "Can't risk losing a genius
to the Magog," and then slipped in a sly, "or you, either."

She heard his startled burst of a laugh. "Yeah. Okay. Got
your point. Find anything interesting, though, you call me
right away."

"You got it," Beka said.

It turned out to be almost alarmingly easy to enter the Magog
ship. The side that it had presented to *Andromeda* hadn't revealed the full extent of the damage, but as their little scout
ship circled it, Beka let out an involuntary gasp. As a pilot, she
couldn't help but wince at the sight of any damaged ship, en-

emy vessel or no. Part of the far side had buckled under what must have been more stress than it had been designed to handle, and then had exploded out.

It must have taken out half the crew with it.

"There's our doorway," Tyr muttered.

Trust a Nietzschean to be utterly pragmatic about it.

The breach was large enough to hold their scout. Beka landed the scout ship inside the Magog vessel with delicate care, not wanting to risk making the breach any worse and endangering both vessels—or trapping them inside if they needed a hasty exit. She and the two men agreed without needing to exchange a word that protective suits were definitely in the picture: There might be little or no breathable atmosphere left in the rest of the Magog ship.

Even with the suit providing her with a steady supply of air, Beka found that she'd been holding her breath as she stepped out into the Magog ship. She let out that breath in a gusty sigh, telling herself not to be a fool. It was dark in here, which was not surprising, Beka thought, since light in all but essential areas would hardly be high on the list of essentials in a damaged ship.

Switching on her suit's light, she pointed. There, a sealed door. It was surprisingly easy to find and work the security latch that reopened it.

Well, sorry, Harper, Beka thought, *but so far this seems to indicate that it's going to be unlikely we'll find any new technology for you.*

What they did find were Magog bodies in the corridor on

the other side of the door. Suffocated Magog lying where they'd fallen, some in convulsions, some looking as if they'd merely lain down to sleep. Beka glanced at Captain Hund, and saw his face twisted with horror.

"Never seen any dead bodies before?" she asked.

"Never so many . . . and certainly never any that are so—hideous."

"You've seen Bem. That should have given you a clue."

"True. But he's only one, and a kind heart. These are—ugly and pathetic in one. And yet, and yet . . . they are still, were still, living beings . . ." He stopped, shaking his head in confusion.

Having a problem, are we? Beka wondered. *Bet it's quite a severe inner battle going on between your morality and your esthetics!*

Just when she was thinking that it would be better for everyone if morality lost this round, Captain Hund shuddered and said, "I have to accept this. If your Reverend Bem can be both ugly and a truly holy soul at the same time, so can these . . . people be both ugly and good."

Wrong decision. Really wrong. "Captain Hund," Beka began, "I don't want to upset you, and I appreciate that you can see Bem for the good soul he is, but he's the exception to the Magog rule—"

"Look at this," Tyr said suddenly, his voice grim.

Beka looked. Oh, damn. This chamber was clearly the Magog idea of a larder, presumably originally refrigerated—or else the Magog liked their midnight snacks a bit ripe—with body parts from various species hanging on hooks everywhere.

One of those species, she recognized with a little shiver of disgust, had been human.

"My God." That was Captain Hund. "Oh my dear God. They . . ." He broke off, face contorted.

"If you need to vomit," Beka said calmly, "be sure to use the suit's emergency tube, there to the left of your face. Don't clog up your faceplate or you'll choke yourself."

He didn't do any of that. But judging from his greenish hue, it had been a near thing.

Tyr was still exploring. "Brace yourself, Captain," he said harshly. "It's going to get worse. A lot worse."

"What do you—oh. Oh God, what . . ."

Hund fell back against a wall, and this time was clearly fighting a battle just to keep from passing out. Beka glanced past him, and had to fight her own battle not to be sick. The Magog had left two of their hosts here, or maybe the hosts had come here in one last, vain attempt to escape. Too late for any escape, because the frantic Magog young, suffocating as their hosts suffocated, had fought their way half out of their dying hosts, who lay torn and contorted in their death agonies, only to die themselves from the lack of air.

"Evil . . ." That was Captain Hund. "They are evil. Utterly, utterly evil. We must destroy them all."

Told you so, Beka thought. *Wouldn't believe me, would you?* "Yes, well, now that we're here, let's check out the rest of the ship first, just in case there really is someone still alive."

"They don't deserve to live."

"Maybe, maybe not, but let's just check things out first."

Beka pointed. "Their version of a command deck should be this way. But the odds are good that," she paused, checking her instruments, "mm, yes. The odds are more than good that the greatest concentration of air is there, too. Which means living Magog. And we don't know if they're conscious or not."

"Won't matter," Tyr said tersely.

They headed warily on down the dark corridor. The suit muffled all outside sounds, leaving Beka only the sound of her own breathing in her headphones and, more faintly, the breathing of Hund and Tyr. This dark, empty place was starting to get to her, or maybe just getting to be a little too much like every one of those stupid old horror vids she'd enjoyed as a kid.

Yeah, the ones in which idiot explorers find out that an abandoned ship isn't empty after all, and something jumps out of the shadows—

Something did. Instead of screaming like those idiot explorers, Beka fired at pointblank range. The Magog collapsed at her feet and lay twitching. Tyr put another shot into its head with professional precision, and the Magog lay still.

Never did like those horror vids. Not once I grew up. "Well, now we know," Beka said. "Just as Rommie said, not all the ship's airless. Not completely, anyhow."

Another shadow darted across her vision, but was gone before she could get off a shot at it. "Uh-huh," Beka said. "They're definitely not all dead. Guys, I vote for a careful retreat."

"Seconded," Tyr agreed. "We don't know what's ahead of us, and blind assaults are a waste of personnel."

"But we can't just retreat," Captain Hund began. "We have to destroy all of those—"

"We have to survive first," Tyr countered brusquely, and gave him a shove in the right direction.

Just then the Magog gave proof positive that at least some of them had suits. Five of them, bulky in those suits but as swift as ever, came rushing down the corridor after them. Tyr calmly shot the one in the lead, shattering its faceplate and head in a revolting fountain. The others, not at all put off by their comrade's death, clambered over the fallen body.

Tyr summed it up. "Run!"

They raced for the scout ship, Beka herding Captain Hund in front of her in case he tried anything stupidly heroic or just plain stupid. "Go on, move it! Get on board!"

She practically shoved Hund into the ship and into his seat and started powering up. "Come on, Tyr! Get up here!"

He got off several skillful shots designed to cause the most chaos in a closed corridor, and dove into the scout in a swift forward roll even as Beka started sealing the door. "Hang on," she cried, "we're going out!"

She sent the little scout shooting away from the Magog ship. Rommie's voice came over her headphones, warning, "The Magog have just sent all Life Support to their Command Deck, and all power to their weaponry."

"Gotcha, Rommie," Beka said. "We're coming home as fast as I can get this ship to go."

"They're firing," Tyr said laconically.

"Hang on!"

Beka sent the maneuverable little scout into a series of eva-sive twists and turns. A hot white blaze of power cut across her field of vision, dazzling her. A miss, though, that was a clean miss, and as soon as her vision cleared—

"Firing again."

"Tyr, I can't see! Grab the controls!"

"Rommie," Captain Hund commanded, and for once his voice was cold and crisp, an officer's voice. "We need protec-tive fire. Now!"

"You got it!" That was Harper's ever-cheerful voice.

Sure enough, a fierce barrage from Rommie's weapon bank hit the Magog ship fore and aft. Already badly overstressed, its fuselage blew apart into a blazing storm of fragments.

"Watch out!"

One metallic shard, as sharp and narrow as a spear, stabbed into the scout. Fortunately, its own width almost completely blocked up the hole it had made, enough so to keep the scout from breaking open, but its point slashed right across Beka's faceplate.

It's cracked! The faceplate's going to break open and I'm going to die, because this ship's losing air—

"Open your faceplate," Captain Hund commanded.

"What—"

"Just do it, damn it!"

What the hell, she had nothing else she could do. Beka opened the broken faceplate, and Hund, opening his, promptly sealed the two faces of their suits together. She froze, afraid to move lest she break the precarious seal, but Hund, his face so close to hers that she would go cross-eyed if she tried to focus, grinned at her, a very Dylan-like grin.

And it's just the sort of crazy chivalry our Dylan would pull!

As she and Hund shared their air and kept from moving as best they could, Tyr brought the wounded scout safely back aboard *Andromeda Ascendant.*

"You two can break up the embrace," he said dryly. "We're here."

Back on the Command Deck, Captain Hund lost any humor he'd shown aboard the scout. Instead, he was grim and silent from the violence he'd witnessed. He had, Beka thought, forcibly grown up.

"I have to thank you for the air," she said.

"I could hardly have let you die." He paused for just a moment, and then added, "You are a worthy member of this *Andromeda*'s crew."

"I . . . well. Thank you."

"And now," he began, but never got to finish.

At that moment, Rommie cut in with, "Everyone strap in. The anomaly zone is reopening."

It did, with a sudden blaze of shifting color and shape, and the ship shook wildly. Beka forgot about gratitude to Hund and grabbed for the controls, struggling to hold *Andromeda* steady.

Not now, not just when I find out that Daylan Hund has some unexpected depths to him—

But the now-familiar blue-white light enveloped him. And—

—he was gone—

—and a new figure was there in his place.

Unfortunately, it wasn't Dylan. It wasn't even saurian.

This time the transferred captain that they'd received was truly . . . alien.

SEVENTEEN • WE MAY BE BETTER STRANGERS

> If a man be gracious and courteous to strangers, it
> shows he is a citizen of the world.
>
> —FRANCIS BACON
>
> Make that, rather, of the universe.
>
> —DYLAN HUNT

Good Lord, Dylan thought in utter astonishment. And, *Good Lord*, again, too stunned for much else.

Oh, it was really fortunate that he hadn't blacked out during *this* transfer! Actually, it was amazing that he'd even managed to stay on his feet with the shock of it. Just when he'd been about to be murdered by the former pacifists, he was—was very much elsewhere. Yes, and in a once-neat uniform that was now stained with human and Magog blood. What an elegant figure.

He needed all his wits about him right now, because this was most definitely not his right dimension, and no, "alien" didn't even begin to cover it. It had been a bad enough shock to turn up in the middle of the saurians, but they, at least, had been still understandable as evolutionary alternates of mammals.

And they'd been downright first cousins to humanity when compared to these guys.

The group facing him did look vaguely human, which made the whole thing all that much alarming—they were biped, one head, no scales or anything like that. But they all looked exactly alike, like a roomful of clones, and they all were completely androgynous, with not even a clue as to gender. The beings' faces were just a touch too narrow, too oval, and were dead white in a way that said this wasn't mere albinism but the norm for their kind. Their noses and ears were mere slits. And their eyes, which had no white to them at all and were all a clear, eerie indigo, took up almost half of their faces.

There was also that little thing about their arms. Which were longer than those of any human and which had two, not one, elbows in each arm. Their fingers were longer than human fingers, too, with too many bends in them. And they were all as hairless as so many eggs.

Any other oddnesses about their shapes—and Dylan suspected there were many, were hidden by their loose, flowing floor-length tunics of some stiff, dull blue fabric—and all of those were identical, too.

They were in the middle of what Dylan assumed was an alternate Command Deck—one that was all a stainless, sterile white.

Uh . . . huh, Dylan thought. *Even for an alternate dimension, this one is really weird. And I never thought that anything else could make the saurians and their lousy decorating sense seem downright homey!*

At least the anomalies seemed to have decided to shut down pretty quickly. The ship rode steadily in undisturbed space.

Someone needed to say something quickly, and as the new arrival, it had better be him. "First of all, can you understand me?"

"Understand." The one word didn't seem to come from any one of them in particular.

"Ah, good." He was definitely caught in a "talk fast" situation. "As you can plainly see," Dylan began, "I'm not your regular captain."

"Clear."

"Is, yes. Not our captain-leader-clan."

"Single-mind?"

Their voices sounded absolutely identical—flat and empty of recognizable emotion.

"I, uh, think the answer is yes. I'm a single entity."

"Need head of clan here, must be, but is not."

"Yes, I know." *At least I think I figured out what you just said.* "I am not in my right place, either." Aware from their hesitant and awkward wordings that they weren't speaking their native language, Dylan spoke slowly and as clearly as possible. "Do you know what happened? Did you just experience a zone of anomalies? Strange colors and shapes in space?"

"Is-was."

He'd take that for a yes, past tense. "The anomaly zone has

done this before," Dylan told them. "It seems determined to keep switching me with other captains."

"Captain-leader? Ship other clan?"

"Uh, yes, that's right." *I think.* "I'm the captain-leader of the ship named the *Andromeda Ascendant.* That's where your captain, uh, captain-leader-clan probably is right now."

"Human?"

Their voices still registered no recognizable emotions. But somehow something in their tone and that flat, unblinking indigo stare still managed to send a warning prickle up Dylan's spine.

"*Other* human," he answered evasively.

They broke off speaking to him, clustering together and whispering busily. What Dylan could hear of them wasn't reassuring. They all sounded exactly alike, and what he assumed was their native language sounded to him almost like the clicks and whirrs of insects.

I think I've got it. They're not mammals or saurians. No, I'll bet anything that these guys, no matter how almost-humanoid they may look, are actually an insectoid species.

That would explain their clonelike similarity and their utter androgyny: They were hatchlings—larvae?—from the same hive. If he was right and these folks really were insect-types, these could well be the drones, the workers, going out into space as expendable explorers while the—well, might as well stay with the insect theme—while their queen stayed safely at home.

Well, at least he wasn't . . . what was the word? Entomophobic, that was it, afraid of insects. Dealing with intelligent insects wouldn't be a problem for him, since the main issue was intelligence, not species.

But this was the first time he'd landed among people who weren't even vaguely related to human. Was this really a parallel dimension? Or had he suddenly been thrown, so to speak, out of the loop altogether? God, if that had happened, if he was forever trapped out here—

No, no, wait, panic doesn't solve anything. The saurians weren't mammals, but they were still parallels of humanity living on a parallel of Andromeda. *That's the constant:* Andromeda. *Yes, that's right, and the Gandhians, for all their overwhelming prettiness, were also pretty obvious parallels, too, and so was their . . . Andi.*

Then, if this ship turned out to be some sort of alternate *Andromeda*, it meant that he was still safe. Relatively safe at any rate.

"Hello?" Dylan began tentatively. "We need to talk."

All those bald white heads turned to him at precisely the same time, in precisely the same smooth movement, and all those too-large indigo eyes staring unblinkingly at him.

"I'm sorry that I don't speak your language," Dylan continued, "but I'm sure you understand that I really can't do anything about it right now."

No answer.

"So if you don't mind speaking the language that I do know, we can do something about this—"

There was absolutely no warning. They were motionless— and in the next instant they were swarming closely around him, still expressionless.

"Uh, folks, I don't understand. Is this a threat or a greeting?"

They were . . . sniffing him?

"Right now, I don't think I smell all that good. And this blood, well, it's not mine, but—"

To Dylan's alarm, one of them suddenly shot out a long, narrow blue tongue and tapped his check with it. Tasting him?

"Sorry, but I don't kiss on the first date."

Just as suddenly, they swarmed back from him to the far side of the Command Deck, clicking and whirring to each other.

"Let me guess: I don't smell or taste quite like a proper human from this dimension."

"You are not vermin," they said.

What did you say to that? "Well, ah, thank you," Dylan said warily.

"You fail to one-mind-group understand. You, single-mind human are. But not vermin."

That seemed to be an important distinction to them. However, if that meant that they saw some or most humans as vermin . . . that was not good. Not good at all. And about that "single-mind" comment . . . these people were a group-mind? Some insects were, after all.

"Not vermin," Dylan agreed emphatically. "Does your ship have a name?"

Blank stares.

"You know," he tried again, "a distinguishing, uh, sound that means it, specifically? Anything that sounds like *Andromeda*?"

"Ship-hive *A'i-dro'oam'd'a*."

A shock of renewed hope blazed through him. "That's wonderful!" Dylan exclaimed. "I, uh, mean, that's an excellent name. For a ship-hive." *And it's definitely a variation of* Andromeda. *Which means that weird though this all is, it* is *still a parallel dimension. I still do have a chance to get home.*

"Human not vermin," the aliens repeated. "Single-mind. Need communication bettering. Need history bettering."

"Yes, I agree, but I—whoa, wait, what are you doing?"

They were moving toward him as one, more slowly and purposefully this time. And this time Dylan was sure that he caught a definite sense of menace in their relentless approach.

"Must be of us if captain-leader-clan."

"You know," he said, backing up, "I don't think I like the sound of that. I think I'd rather stay as I am, thank you very much."

The swarm was between him and the Command Deck door. No way out. But as he backed up, Dylan hastily glanced sideways, orienting himself. Multijointed though those alien fingers might be, they were still fingers. The controls couldn't be all that different . . . and if that were true, then those were . . .

Dylan dove for the console. Indentations instead of buttons, but he could still hit them—

Yes! The ship lurched wildly as he hit the right controls, catching the aliens off guard. But they didn't fall, just slid together into a tighter group with a smoothness that told Dylan that their . . . legs were definitely alien.

"All right, as you see, I hold the pilot's console. Storm me, and I'll send the lot of you crashing into the ceiling."

"Wanting what, you?"

"Wanting a chance to talk this out," Dylan countered. "No threats from anyone. All right?"

"Human can not captain-leader be, ship."

"Not on one of your, uh, ship-hives, I understand that. Believe me, I'm very well aware that I'm an alien species on this ship. But right now, the fact remains that, human or no, I'm the only captain-leader you have."

"Not."

"Sorry, but it's true. Do you people understand the concept of parallel dimensions? More than one reality?" He waited a moment to see if they got that. "Yes? Good. Then you also have to understand that if you want your own captain-leader back again, you really don't want to damage me. There has to be a balance, one captain per dimension, before there can be a transfer."

He was getting pretty good at rattling that theory off, yes and making it sound like utter fact. Which by now he really hoped it was.

There was a great deal of that whispered chittering among them.

"Not knowing captain-leader being human," they finally said. "Not knowing human not-vermin other existed."

"Yes, well, I didn't know that you folks existed, either. The universe—universes, rather, are a never-ending source of amazement, aren't they?"

Blank stares.

Dylan sighed. "Never mind."

"You, single-mind, must know the history."

"Not into never-ending sources of amazement, I take it?"

"Must know the history."

"Well, yes, since I am here, it seems only reasonable that I learn something about your history. But we do have this little problem with communication. And so I don't see how . . . hey, what are you—no!"

They'd swarmed him again, moving with that unnerving hive-mind speed and precision. Before Dylan could pull away, two of them managed to jam what looked like an army helmet with weird circuitry on its sides onto his head. Dylan struggled, trying to tear it off—but suddenly he couldn't manage to move at all as images started flooding into his brain . . .

He saw a familiar blue world hanging in space . . . It was Earth, humanity's homeworld . . .

But this was an Earth of long centuries ago . . . he knew that fact without knowing how he did . . .

But more and more facts were pouring into his mind, overwhelming his resistance, forcing him to know . . .

Yes, this was Earth, an alternate planet, strangely lacking in what he knew of his dimension's past.

Yes, he saw Slipstream technology arrive to open up the universe to humanity. Dylan saw Nietzscheans gathering in secret, planning their program of enhancement and improvement of their genome—and then leaving Earth to found their colonies away from the "inferior" humans.

But then Dylan saw Earth make a fatal mistake. In this dimension, there was a strong separatist movement ruling the

planet's politics, and so Earth refused to join the Commonwealth.

Then the aliens came, this insectoid species, the invaders, the
hive-ancestors of these beings. Isolated from the Commonwealth, Earth stood alone. The invaders swept away all resistance, but saw it only as cleaning away the vermin. Their minds
were too different. They saw no signs that humanity bore intelligence. They saw all the buildings as mere hive-dwellings, all the
art and music as so much meaningless shape and noise—they saw
only vermin, and they exterminated vermin.

Not my world, Dylan thought, fighting this false reality, *not
my people, not my dimension, not my history!*

Dylan clung to those thoughts, struggling to pull himself
free.

But now he saw this ship being built, this alternate *Andromeda* designed exactly as his own ship was planned—but built by
the last humans, the prisoners that the aliens thought had a
touch of sentience to them.

No! He had to break out of this!

The prisoners who were then casually exterminated when
their work was completed.

No! These beings were too alien, these beings saw humans
as vermin, they knew nothing about him, and that put him into
incredible peril—

He was in peril right now! The device was too alien, the images too alien for a human mind—

"Enough of this!" Dylan cried, hearing his voice sounding

far away and tinny, and with a great effort, tore the helmet from his head.

The aliens snatched the helmet from him as Dylan fell to his knees. As he struggled to get back to his feet, his head pounding, the aliens did one of their group slides back across the room again.

"Vermin behavior," they told him.

"What?" He finally made it back up again, fighting not to sway. "Not wanting to have my brain damaged by alien technology is a bad thing?"

"Vermin behavior."

"Your ancestors destroyed the humans of this dimension. Now, *that* seems like pretty bad behavior to me."

"Vermin-cleansing it was."

With great restraint, Dylan told them, "I won't argue about the past. I wasn't there and neither were you."

"The human does not have history."

Damn it! "I do have history, my people have history, and my ship has history. It just isn't *this* history! I am not of this dimension, and you have already agreed that I am not vermin." Dylan's head still hurt, he was tired, and he was in no mood to be politic. "So let's stop this nonsense, all right? We don't need to talk about the past. We need to concentrate on the here-and-now."

"Denying history."

"No! I'm not denying anyone's history. All I'm saying is that we need to get your captain-leader-whatever back here and me back to my right dimension!"

"Making vermin-loud noises."

Damn it, he must have just hit one of their species' taboos. They apparently never raised their voices. He really didn't need to have another complication added to an already complicated situation. It was an effort, but Dylan forced himself to say more quietly, "I'm sorry if I just broke one of your customs. Please forgive it and mark it up to my being a stranger here."

"Stranger."

Damn it again! It was beginning to seem as though these people seemed determined to take everything the wrong way.

Oh. Hell. Maybe they were. After all, their ancestors had seen humans as vermin—Maybe their species were all xenophobes, afraid of and hostile towards strangers.

"Not-of-hive," they continued. "Dangerous."

The whisper spread through the group. "Dangerous."

It's xenophobia, all right. They can't accept any intelligence but their own.

Dylan was still stuck on this ship, though, which meant that he still had to keep trying to get through to them. "No, please understand. I am not dangerous to you. I don't mean any of you any harm."

"Single-mind. Stranger. Dangerous."

"Look, all we can do right now is to accept that we are two different species and that we don't know each other's customs. Do you agree?"

"There are no customs. Not from humans."

"Look, let's just back off a minute and think this over. No need to do anything any of us might regret."

But while Dylan was saying these easy words, all the while never taking his glance from the swarm, he was blindly hunting for the right controls. Ha, yes, he had them.

"Human. Stranger. Dangerous."

"There's no getting through to you, is there? You just can't accept that I'm a sentient being."

They just stared.

"Hell. I was right. You can't."

They started toward him, and this time there was no doubt about the casual menace in their bearing. Dylan was a problem to the hive, and problems to the hive were, in true insect fashion, to be removed.

He punched down, hitting the control he wanted. Sure enough, the ship yawed sharply to one side, and the swarm slid sideways.

Now!

Dylan, pushing off from the console, hit the deck running, and was through the Command Deck door before they could recover. Nowhere to go, but at least there was a whole ship in which to—to do what? Survive.

Dylan Hunt, fugitive.

And how the hell do I get out of this mess?

EIGHTEEN • DYLAN ON THE RUN

Of all escape mechanisms, death is the most efficient.
But I'll settle for the second most efficient means,
thank you very much.

—GENERAL ADAIN "ESCAPE ARTIST" SERVAL,
CV 1056

Dylan raced down the ship's corridors, searching frantically for any and all familiar parallels to his own ship, looking for any place in which he could hide, make a real plan, or at least defend himself against the enemy, all the while hearing the whispering sound of those blue robes dragging against the floor as the aliens pursued him.

Damn it, this was a ridiculous situation! Here he was being hunted through a closed environment, a ship in the middle of open space. And he couldn't even use one of the rescue pods to escape—assuming that he could find them, assuming that these guys even bothered with rescue pods—since he had to be here for when the anomaly zone reopened.

Yes, and how he was going to manage to get back onto the Command Deck to wait for the anomaly zone to reopen without these guys killing him was yet another problem—

Uh-oh. First things first. Another cluster of the aliens stood in the corridor ahead of him. This new group looked absolutely identical to the aliens he'd seen on the Command Deck—and all of the aliens, Dylan knew, were joined into the group mind. That meant that as soon as one of them saw him, they all knew where he was. In another second, they were going to get the message from his pursuers, and he'd be caught between them.

This is getting better and better by the moment.

A new corridor opened up on his left. Dylan ducked into it before any of the new group turned his way. They'd all be after him in a moment, but maybe he could find a place to hide. . . .

Ah, yes, this corridor should lead to the Hydroponics Deck . . . Dylan hoped. It would probably be there in some form. Presumably these guys needed veggies in their diets, too, even if he hadn't seen their dentition, assuming of course that they even had teeth. . . .

Yes, it was the Hydroponics Deck, not all that different from the one he knew, even if he didn't recognize all the plants. There were plenty of places to hide in here. Dylan dropped to his hands and knees and wriggled under something that had long, thick fronds that swept the floor. Yes, it was like a green cave in here, a perfect space for curling up and trying to silently catching his breath, and start making at least a tentative plan.

They haven't sounded any alarms.

Of course they haven't, he answered himself. *Why bother, since they know that one of them is bound to see me sooner or later? And they know that I can't get off this ship.*

He heard the hiss of robes. Sure enough, the aliens had reached the Hydroponics Deck. Wasn't it going to dawn on them that they should stop and search? Would they just keep going? Would he be that lucky?

No, he wouldn't. They had stopped and were methodically searching through every plant, under every table, in every bin. It was, Dylan thought grimly, just a matter of time before they found him.

All right, then, let 'em.

Dylan edged away very slowly, waiting . . .

Now!

He leaped out of hiding and grabbed the nearest alien, one arm going around the alien's throat, the other pinning those extra-jointed arms to the being's sides. Limbs that weren't at all human limbs flailed at him, but Dylan just tightened his grip. Even these guys had to breathe, and the alien went limply docile.

"I don't want to hurt him," Dylan said.

"It does not matter," the others said. "One unit can be sacrificed."

Good God! They're going to kill us both!

As the others calmly fired at their comrade, Dylan dove clear. He rolled, leaped back to his feet, and took out the closest alien with a sharp kick. No time to see what damage he'd done. Dylan leaped over the fallen being, dodged as the others grabbed at him, and raced on down the length of the Hydroponics Deck.

Hell, more of them, coming straight at him. Dylan leaped up, caught one of the banks of overhead lights, and pulled himself up onto a narrow catwalk. Two of the more athletic aliens followed him. Not the best place for a fight, but you couldn't always choose your site.

What you could choose, however—

Dylan grinned. Tyr was right. Anything could be a weapon, all right. Ahead was what looked very much like a coconut tree, full of hard-husked fruit. He grabbed a coconut and hurled it like a football. It smashed into the lead alien's face and the being fell from the catwalk. The second alien ducked, but Dylan's second coconut caught it a glancing blow. Dylan finished the job with a hard shove, sending that one crashing down as well, and then hurried down the length of the catwalk.

Of course more aliens were waiting for him down there, their weapons ready. Dylan deliberately jumped down into the middle of them before they could fire, knocking three over with the force of his landing, and blindly ran before they could untangle themselves.

Too bad I couldn't get one of their weapons!

But yes, here, a corridor, and a bend in it—damn, he could hear more aliens coming from the far end. And others were behind him.

A control panel . . . there has to be a control panel somewhere along the bottom of a wall, somewhere along here—

Ha, yes!

Kneeling, teeth gritted with the effort, Dylan manhandled the panel open more by sheer will than anything else, and then forced himself into the tiny opening behind it, pulling the panel shut again behind him. Not much room to maneuver in here, not much he could do but just stay still, holding his breath and waiting . . . waiting . . . hearing the whisper of blue robes passing by outside.

All right, the corridor was clear at last. Dylan stepped silently back out from hiding, just as silently pushing the panel back into place.

But I can't keep galloping around the ship forever. Sooner or later someone's going to corner me.

Whoa, wait. He'd seen this version of *Andromeda* being built when the aliens had forced that helmet-technology on him. There'd already been the control panel pretty much where he'd expected it and the Hydroponics Deck where it should be. And unless there'd been some pretty drastic retro-fitting in the three hundred years of its existence, which wasn't too likely, this ship was going to continue to be a very close parallel to his own . . .

Dylan did some hasty overhead scouting. Oh yes. Every ship of any size had almost a second city's worth of engineering and ventilation shafts, a veritable maze with plenty of access panels, since the engineers would need to get to any damage as quickly and efficiently as possible. Unfortunately, he wouldn't be able to get back into the Command Deck that way. For obvious reasons of security, the Command Deck had its own separate ventilation system. But just about everywhere else on the ship would be open to him.

There was one of the panels, set high on one wall. Reachable, yes, and if . . . he . . . could . . . only . . . get it . . . open—

Curse it! The panel had just come open, but with a screech that sounded to him as loud as a sheet of metal being torn in half.

A noise that's guaranteed to bring every alien within earshot running.

Dylan hastily grabbed the edge of the opening and hoisted himself up and into it, pulling the noisy panel shut again. Bent over in the narrow confines, he hurried on down the shaft as quickly as possible, trying at the same time to make as little noise as possible. He knew every inch of his *Andromeda*, and he'd just have to keep believing that the layout here was exactly the same.

Yes, yes, it was, because here was the marked intersection of Shaft 4C with 3G. Left turn, and hurry on down 3G, and never mind that it was close and hot in here and he couldn't straighten up. There was air, he wouldn't suffocate, and he could endure the closeness and low ceiling.

All right, here was the slope leading down to the Officers' Mess. Dylan went flat when he was directly over it, hearing faint sounds from down there. Ear to the floor of the shaft, he followed the procession of aliens . . . Forget the Officers' Mess. Too many of them were heading this way.

The shaft was too narrow to let him turn around. Dylan carefully backed out, trying not to let his mind go overactive and imagine someone lying in wait for him. No one there, of course, though it was just a matter of time before someone figured out he'd gone up here.

And then it boils down to who knows this maze better.

Right turn, climb up a small slope, blessing his training of three hundred years ago that had insisted every officer memorize every inch of his ship. Even if this wasn't his ship, not exactly.

Now, up this narrow ladder . . . all those years of ship development, and no one had figured out a better way to do this . . . and here was the level of the next deck. The Medical Deck, if he hadn't gotten turned around.

Ah yes, this was the Medical Deck, all right, spotlessly clean and absolutely white. More important, there was no one in it.

Yet.

Dylan forced open another panel. This one obliged him by not screeching, and Dylan swung soundlessly down out of the vent. There should be something useful here, assuming that he could get into one of the cabinets.

Ah, yes, a flaw at last. Someone hadn't been too careful about locking up this drawer. Dylan rummaged hastily through various medical tools . . . blast, nothing useful, nothing with a point or an edge—

Ha! He snatched up a scalpel—at least, that was what he assumed it was. It had a sharp blade, at any rate, better than nothing. It would be nice if there was something with a little more firepower, but you took what you could get—

The faintest whisper of a sound warned him. Dylan whirled just in time, seeing the alien with weapon ready to fire, and lunged, his left arm knocking the weapon aside, his right hand driving the scalpel home with practiced ease. The alien crumpled without a sound.

Yes, but now they all know where I am. And they're not going to make the mistake of walking alone again.

Hurry back to the open panel, climb back up into the ventilation shaft and get away from there as fast as his crouched-over position would allow him to run. Right turn, head down this slope, left turn, go straight ahead for quite a while, this way taking him back over the Hydroponics Deck. Dylan toyed with stopping there again, since there was a convenient panel at this point—no, forget that, there were several aliens passing through there . . .

On second thought . . .

He got the panel open, slid silently down, neatly cut the throat of the last alien so that there'd be no sound, then hoisted himself back up, closed the panel and hurried on down the vent. Behind him, down there on the floor of the corridor, the others would have realized what had just happened. Too bad. When you were one against many, guerrilla warfare was about the only way to go.

Dylan paused at another panel, listening. One . . . two aliens.

Only two? That was a big mistake on their part, underestimating him. If he timed this just right, and the panel actually cooperated . . . yes. It slid open with almost alarming ease, and Dylan leaped down. He hit both aliens squarely, knocking them down. No false niceties or worries about morality here. Dylan killed both before they could even register what was happening, then grabbed the weapon from one of them, and swung back up into the vent.

Better, he thought, quickly checking the weapon over, *much better.*

Onward, hastily, down another narrow ladder, left, left again. Stopped at a panel, he heard a whole crowd go by, too many for him to tackle. They were learning: He was too dangerous for them not to hunt in a pack.

Just a matter of time before someone joins me up here, though.

All right, never mind worrying about what hadn't happened yet. He hurried on down a straightaway, and then made a right, a left, another right . . . below him should be one of the Machine Shops. Dylan dared move a panel aside a crack. Yes. Right on target. No one was in it, so he dared to drop down, hunting for anything useful.

Nothing. The sterile white place was as clean as if it had never been used.

He turned—and found himself facing an ambush. Five aliens, five weapons pointed straight at him.

Dylan dropped. The blasts went over him, and he pushed off from the floor, tackling the nearest alien, twisting about, dropping a second with a blast from his stolen gun, rolling free, firing as he went—got another. The remaining two were trying to fire at him, but he kept the bodies between him and them, and the bodies absorbed the blasts. The alien he'd tackled was starting to get back up, but Dylan grabbed him—and the aliens' blasts hit their own instead. The body toppled toward them, and Dylan used it as a shield and got off two more quick shots.

Got them. All five. Tyr would be impressed.

Or maybe not. He'd probably just mutter something about my poor technique.

Dylan hoisted himself back up into the vent and pulled the panel back in place. For a moment, all he could do was lie there, panting and shaken. Had he really just taken out five enemies?

But no, he needed to get out of there, and fast, because the other aliens would already know what had just happened.

Down a slope, left turn, left turn, straightaway . . . he had to stop now, take a rest, wishing he had something cold to drink. Might as well wish for a polite servant to bring it to him as well.

Dylan sighed soundlessly. *All right, enough resting. Onward.*

Which way hadn't he been for a time? Up again, to the right, up again, to the right—

Yes. He was now right over another Machine Shop. This one looked as clean, as white, and as empty as the first—this time genuinely empty. Dylan pried the panel all the way open and dropped lightly down, going into a wary fighting crouch, then relaxing. There really wasn't an alien in sight or, for that matter, in hiding. He had a few moments free to stretch and figure out where to next take his guerrilla war. He quickly locked the Machine Shop's door, then stood back with a weary sigh. God, what he'd do for a real rest.

What if the anomaly zone doesn't reopen within a short time? How long can I keep this one-man war going?

All right. Dylan made a hasty deal with himself. If the anomalies didn't return within a few days, and he knew he was running out of hope, he'd get to an escape pod and try to make a life for himself in this dimension.

Let it not come to that!

What—where—oh. One of the ship's consoles had been accidentally left on by whatever alien had last been in here. Dylan hadn't a clue as to what the buzzing and clicking language meant, but the visual left him no doubt at all.

Here, with a really abysmal sense of timing, came this dimension's version of mysterious enemy attackers.

I wonder who they are in this dimension. And is there anything I can do about the situation?

Something about those ships looked familiar. Dylan racked his tired brains . . . he'd seen them before . . .

Oh, yes! He certainly had seen them before, in his own dimension. These attackers were Nietzscheans.

I never thought that I'd be glad to see that lot! But at least it means that some *humans, or some* form *of humans are still alive and free.*

Now, wasn't this placing him in a weird predicament? If he aided the Nietzscheans, Dylan thought, he would be giving them the information they needed to blow this ship out of space—and himself with it. If he said nothing—

Hell, what difference did it make? The aliens meant to kill

him anyhow. There was no guarantee that the anomaly zone would reopen in time for a rescue, or even reopen at all. He might as well side with at least a type of humanity.

Dylan quickly opened a communications channel, knowing he would have only a few moments before the aliens realized he was sending, and found out where he was. "This is Captain Dylan Hunt," he sent, "and yes, I am, as you see, human. More than that, you don't need to know. Now, listen. I don't have much time before these guys discover me . . ."

When he had finished, the strong-faced woman on the other end of the communication said, "We will consider it. You have an hour to find a way off this ship. After that, we shall destroy it."

Good enough, Dylan thought. He was getting really fed up with this endless guerrilla war, anyhow. In an hour—

Or less. A preliminary shuddering of the ship sent a wild blaze of hope through Dylan. The anomaly zone? Oh let it be the anomaly zone!

The aliens were at the door, and the lock wasn't going to keep them out for more than a few moments. Dylan hurried to the open panel and the ventilation vent—

An alien face looked impassively back at him.

Oh well. I didn't really want to go back in there anyhow.

A quick, desperate idea came to him. No human would fall for this ploy—but these weren't humans.

No other choice. He'd try it.

Dylan turned to face the incoming rush of aliens. "Hi, guys," he said, and raised his stolen weapon. "Shall we dance?"

They'd already had clear evidence of how well he could fight. And they also clearly didn't want to fire on him and be fired upon.

Instead, they swarmed him. "Don't take me back!" Dylan cried. "Don't take me back to the Command Deck! Please! I don't want to go back there!"

They couldn't have understood what was going on, but his apparently genuine panic must have warned them that something was wrong. Did they think he'd planted some type of explosive there? Maybe, maybe not, but they clearly wanted to know just what he had in mind. Sure enough, they dragged him, literally, all the way back to the Command Deck.

"Speak," they said.

"Tell what."

"We kill."

"Well, I already had that part figured out. And I suspect that you're going to kill me no matter what I say or don't say. You do know about those ships out there, I take it?"

"Enemy. You single-mind first."

The ship shook again, more violently this time.

"Have you guys ever heard the story of Brer Rabbit and the Briar Patch?"

The ship shuddered, shuddered again.

"It seems," Dylan continued, "that a farmer caught Brer Rabbit one day and was going to kill him."

The ship slewed sideways. Clinging to a console, Dylan continued, "But Brer Rabbit said to the farmer, 'You can kill me. Just don't throw me into the briar patch. Anything but the briar patch.'"

Blazing color lit up space all around them.

"So the farmer decided to do just that: Throw Brer Rabbit into the briar patch. Well, that was just what Brer Rabbit wanted. 'I was born and bred in a briar patch!'" he said to the farmer.

The aliens got the point. They raised their guns and—

The blue-white light hit him and—

—they fired—

—and he—

—was gone.

NINETEEN · CAPTAIN KAFKA

If you think that the problem is bad now, just wait
until we've solved it.

—EX-SENATOR JEN HARDIN, A.K.A. JEN THE CYNIC,
CV 4181

"Now what in the seven hells," Beka said, "is *that*?"

Oh yes, she was really glad to be rid of pacifistic Captain
Dylan Hund—even if he had turned out to be rather a good
guy once he had been forced to face violence and act like a real
captain—

But what oh what did they have now?

Yes, the . . . creature standing there was biped and yes, the
creature was roughly humanoid in shape—

*But there's no way in hell that this—this—this whatever can be an
alternate Dylan! Can it . . . ?*

The being was man-sized, too, more or less, but with an alien face and form ... big indigo eyes set in a too-narrow dead-white face, no nose but slits, no ears but slits, too many joints in its arms and fingers ... a long, dull blue tunic hid the rest, but Beka suspected that the rest was just as strange.

The alien clearly wasn't exactly happy to be here, either. It kept turning wildly about, as if trying desperately to orient itself.

"Hello?" Beka said tentatively.

The alien turned sharply to her.

So far, so good. "Do you understand me?" Beka asked.

"Hive-not! Vermin!"

Not so good. "Sorry, but I don't get what you're trying to tell us."

"Single-mind? Single-minds? Only? Alone? Single-mind only! Alone! Alone!"

"Hey, take it easy," Beka soothed. "Slow down. It's okay. No one's going to hurt you."

But the alien didn't seem to hear her any more. It kept wildly repeating that panicky, "Alone! Alone!" And then the being slid from that—or any other understandable language—into a series of wild clicks and whirrs that sounded like a hive of hysterical insects and was presumably the alien's native tongue—

And then the alien simply collapsed.

For a stunned moment, everyone just stood staring. Then Beka roused herself and said brightly, "Well, this is different."

Bem and Trance hurried to the crumpled alien's side, examining it together. They murmured together for some time while Beka waited uneasily. At last she couldn't stand the suspense.

"Hello, you two? Hey? Anyone home?"

Trance looked up, her face dreamy-eyed and mystic. "This being is neither mammalian nor reptilian," she said. "Nor, for that matter, is it avian."

"You're kind of limiting the possibilities here, Trance. The alien's what, then? What's left? An insectoid?"

"That does appear to be it," Bem agreed.

"Are you telling me that this version of Dylan is a *bug*?"

"So it seems. But we need to get our, ah, visitor to the Medical Deck so that we can do a genuine examination. This isn't just a brief loss of consciousness," Bem continued, frowning— not a pretty sight on a Magog. "It's not a faint, as we experienced with Captain Hund when he arrived, but a total collapse."

"Disease?" Beka asked in alarm.

"I don't think so."

"No," Trance murmured. "There is neither physical injury nor sickness. But did you not hear that despairing cry of 'single-mind' and that heart-rending repetition of 'alone'? This, I believe, is a hive member who has suddenly been cut off from the group-mind."

Beka stared at her. "Are you saying that he's just gone crazy?"

"We won't know until we can do further testing," Bem said in a voice that allowed for no more discussion. "Tyr, if you could give us a hand . . . ?"

As Beka watched them take the limp figure away, she thought, *Just what we needed. A buggy Dylan.*

Just when I thought that things couldn't possibly get any weirder.

Never tempt the fates, Beka told herself a little later. Things could, as the say went, always get worse. And things plainly hadn't even begun to get as weird as they could get. It was only a short while after the alien had been taken for medical care, and here came an urgent communication from Bem:

"Our patient's gone."

"Do you mean that he's dead?" Beka asked sharply.

"No, I mean gone. Literally."

"But how? Weren't you watching him?"

Tyr cut in, "I delivered him. I wanted to fasten the restraints, keep him under control, but no, these two refused to allow it."

"We feared that his waking up as a prisoner would have driven him completely over the mental edge," Bem said.

Tyr's snort said clearly what he thought of such pampering. "That alien was already over the edge when he arrived. No, what happened was these two took their eyes off him for 'just a few moments,' and our bug took off. Beka, he seems to know this ship as well as we do."

"Hell." That meant that the creature, whatever it was, sane or insane, really was a parallel of Dylan. "Bem, you get back here to the Command Deck, okay? Trance, stay put. Harper, are you there?"

"I heard the whole thing," he said over the communication link. "I'll start tracking."

"Good. Rommie, I assume—"

"I'm on it."

"Okay, then. Tyr, you and me, we're going bug hunting."

Alone, alone.

Single-mind, hive gone.

Hive gone. Hive gone.

Where? What ship-hive?

Not right! Not hive!

Find hive, find group-mind!

Must be here, somewhere, had to be here, somewhere.

Frantic scuttle down corridors. Familiar corridors, that much, yes.

Nothing else the same, everything empty, empty.

Frantic search for safe haven.

Nothing, nothing.

No comfort, no group-mind, just one cut off, one single-mind, impossible, unbearable!

Frantic searching, searching.

Different deck? Not medicine-scent so strong, painful.

Different deck. Yes.

Machine Shop?

Machine Shop. Yes.

Right place, right place, but too cluttered, not right, not hive-part.

No hive.

Hive gone.
Alone—
What—
Alarming! Alarming!
Vermin!

"Vermin!"

Harper nearly jumped out of his skin at that sudden proclamation, whirling about so quickly that he nearly fell off his chair. Recovering, realizing who he was facing, Harper got out a hurried, "Hey, you—uh, gee, you really can move quickly. And quietly, too."

He stared at the alien with a happy mix of curiosity and excitement. Cool, really cool, a whole new species! "Uh, it's okay. You don't have to look at me like that. I won't hurt you. Look, I'm Seamus Harper. Shay-mus. Har-per. Got that? And you are . . . ?"

The alien said nothing, just stared at him with those huge, unblinking indigo eyes. Bug eyes. Literally.

"No? Don't want to give me a name? Or maybe you don't have one? Okay, it doesn't really matter. Uh, wait, you . . . do understand me, don't you?"

"Understand."

"All right, then! Come in, sit down, take a load off your, uh, whatever you've got."

The alien just continued to stare.

"Look, don't worry. I told you, I won't hurt you. Why don't you just make yourself at home? *Mi* Machine Shop, *su* Machine Shop and all that." Harper hit the communications button. "Oh, Beka? Guess who's just come to visit?"

"Hold him there!"

"Yeah. Right."

"Vermin?" the alien repeated, this time more uncertainly.

"Hey, look," Harper said indignantly, "I know this place isn't the neatest in the world, but it's not *that* bad! There's no vermin in here, honest. Nothing personal, but you're the only bug I've seen on this ship."

"Alone . . . alone . . ."

"Yes, I'm the only one in here—oh. Gotcha. You mean that *you're* alone. Yeah, sorry, this all can't be easy for you."

"Not vermin?"

"I already told you that there aren't any—hey! Stop that!"

Without even the slightest warning, the alien suddenly shot forward, touched the tip of its long blue tongue to his cheek, and then retreated again.

Rubbing his cheek, Harper asked, "What was *that*? You tasting me? I'm not good to eat, honest. No, wait, was that, maybe, an analysis? Yeah, I bet that's exactly what it was. You were trying to figure out what I am by the taste of my—my chemistry. I bet you're a hive insect, right, like a bee or an ant."

"Not vermin," the alien said.

"Told you there weren't any—oh, wait, you mean *I'm* not vermin. Well, gee, thanks, fella, I, uh, think.

"Whoa, but if you're a hive insect, that explains why you're doing the 'alone' bit. Geez, you must be *really* alone. I bet I'm right, you are ordinarily a part of a group mind."

"Group-mind! Understanding!"

"And now you're stuck here in a different dimension as a separate entity without a hive anywhere near you. Geez, I can't even imagine what that must feel like. Talk about lost! And—boy, would I love to analyze your brain waves!" Harper leaned forward eagerly. "I, uh, don't suppose you'd let me—"

The alien hissed and sprang back.

"Hey, it's okay." Harper hastily sat back again. "I'm sorry. Didn't mean to alarm you. Hey! No, wait, don't—oh damn."

He hit the communications button again. "Beka, sorry, but our visitor just decided to head on out again."

Not-vermin human?

Possible?

Yes, possible, taste/analysis correct.

True.

Other humans? Here? Not-vermin?

Not right.

Strange, strange.

No hive, wrong ship.

Not ship-hive.

Wrong-familiar.

Not possible.

Alone. Alone.

Frantic hunting.

Not this deck.

Where? Where?

Alone, alone.

Single-mind, no, not right.

Where?

Where?

Hive gone.

No place.

Nothing.

No hope.

Nothing.

Hold on, hold on, hold on.

"There is suddenly an intruder in my ventilation system," Rommie said suddenly. "It can only be our other-dimensional visitor."

"Oh, great," Beka said dourly. "I always wanted to play 'Catch the Alien in the Maze' with a real, live alien. Which way is he heading?"

"It is difficult to keep an accurate track of him. The alien is both very swift and very erratic and illogical in his movements." Rommie paused. "Right now, he would seem to be heading for my Hydroponics Deck. That destination, though, you understand, is subject to change without warning."

"Understood," Beka said. "But hey, it's still better than having no clues at all. Tyr—"

Tyr was already on his way without waiting for the merely human woman to catch up. Beka hurried after him, swearing under her breath about Nietzscheans, aliens, anomaly zones, and just about everything else she could think of. If this really was a parallel Dylan, and if the anomaly zone opened before they could find him and get him back to the Command Deck—hell, she didn't know what would happen then. There was no telling what the alien would do, either, mentally unstable as he was right now. If he managed to get his hands on a weapon . . .

"There he is," Tyr hissed.

The alien was, indeed, there on the Hydroponics Deck, hastily munching on double handfuls of fruit. Right, Beka thought, insectoids would probably need a lot of sugar in their systems to keep their faster metabolisms going.

"Don't scare him," Beka whispered.

"Huh."

Tyr shot forward with Nietzschean speed. But the alien dropped the fruit and leaped straight up—

"Way to go, Tyr!" Beka said. "You scared him right back up into the ventilation system. Tyr—"

But Tyr was already hoisting himself up, going after his prey.

"Damn it," Beka snapped. "Rommie?"

"They are both heading toward the Observation Deck—no, the alien and Tyr have both changed course. Now they are heading back toward . . ."

"Toward? Rommie?"

"They have separated. The alien has dropped down out of the ventilation system into a Machine Shop. Tyr missed the turn and has lost him."

"Oh, that's just wonderful."

"Beka," Rommie said suddenly, "the alien is now headed toward you. I . . . am not certain, but I believe he may be now armed."

"This keeps getting better and better by the moment. Okay, Rommie, warning taken."

She certainly didn't want to get into a fight with the alien. From what Harper had told her, the insectoid was more terrified than vicious, and close to insanity from being torn out of its collective mind. Of course, Harper *was* wrong occasionally. But a crazy alien was going to be a hell of a lot more dangerous and unpredictable than a sane one. And either way, sane or insane alien, Beka really didn't feel like a fight.

Besides, we need the alien alive and well for the next dimension shift!

Whoa, sudden idea. The alien had been almost desperately munching that fruit, but had been interrupted in his frantic feast by Tyr. That meant that the insectoid must really be low on sugar right now.

Sure he was. Why else would he be risking coming back to the Hydroponics Deck so soon?

Sugar he wants. Beka thought, *sugar he gets.*

She began hastily pulling off all the sweetest fruits she could find, and putting them in a glass together, then mashing them up, adding just enough water to make the mess syrupy and drinkable.

Just in time. Here came the alien now. He stopped short at the sight of her, staring at her with those huge blue eyes. And yes, he was armed. During that visit to Harper, he must have palmed a handgun.

Geez.

"Look," Beka said in her gentlest voice. "See? Look what's here. Sugar, sweet, good. See?"

She faked taking a sip. Even the scent of so much concentrated sweetness was revolting, but Beka forced a smile. "Umm. Good. Come, try."

The alien didn't move.

"Okay, look. I'm putting the glass down right here on this ledge. See? It's right here."

She backed off, waiting. The alien took a step forward, another step. And then the being frantically snatched up the glass and drained the entire thing practically in one gulp.

"See? Isn't that—oh hell."

Without a change of expression, the alien raised its gun and fired—

Tyr dropped down on the alien, sending the blast wide, and knocked it out with one quick, efficient blow. "You all right?" he asked tersely.

"Uh, yes. Thank you. You . . . didn't kill him, did you?"

Tyr checked. "No." He bent, slung the limp body over his shoulder, and straightened in one smooth, fluid motion. "Let's get him back to the Command Deck."

"And hope that the anomaly zone reopens soon," Beka finished. "And that Dylan is still alive."

"And that this time," Tyr said, for him almost wearily, "we actually get him back."

TWENTY · UTOPIA LOST AND FOUND

A lot of people spend half their time wishing for things that they could have—if, that is, they didn't spend half their time wishing.

—POET/PHILOSOPHER AERIN HABAND,
"DREAMS AND DELUSIONS," CV 4824

This time around, Dylan knew from the first moment of vague consciousness that he wasn't dead. He also knew that he was lying on a bed, a rather firm, no, downright hard one.

He wasn't so sure about anything else, though, those little things like where he was or in what condition he might be.

At least he didn't seem to hurt anywhere. But the last thing that Dylan remembered clearly was the insectoids firing at him just as the blue-white light had caught him.

Which won out?

Now he was aware of a sharp scent in the air—medicine?

No, more than that. This was the unmistakable hospital aroma of *Andromeda*'s Medical Deck.

"He's waking up," someone said.

"All vital signs seem absolutely normal," another someone said.

Dylan opened his eyes, slowly, warily, the lids feeling heavier than they should. "Now . . . where am I?" he managed, trying to sit up.

"Easy does it," a voice said, and hands pushed him gently back down onto the bed. "Don't rush it. Let your head clear a little more before you even think about getting up."

Dylan blinked, blinked again, trying to get his vision to cooperate. "This . . . is the Medical Deck, isn't it?"

"Yes, it is."

"It's the *Andromeda*'s Medical Deck."

"Yes."

"Then, please don't take this the wrong way, but: Who the hell are you?"

The dark-skinned woman in the medic's uniform grinned at him, her teeth flashing white. "I don't blame you for wondering. I'm Dr. Helena Travis, and no, don't worry, Captain Hunt, you don't know me. All right, do you think you can sit up now?"

He could, albeit a bit more slowly and carefully than he would have liked. "Let me guess," Dylan said, aware now that he was clad in some very soft and comfortable bed clothes. Better than the stark naked surprise of the pacifists' dimension. "This is still not the right dimension."

"Sorry, sir, but no, it's not. But I think you'll like this one a great deal more than the ones you were telling us about."

Dylan frowned. "I don't remember telling anyone—"

"Captain, you were out of your head for a bit. Stress, exhaustion, depleted minerals, dehydration, and—I don't think I need to go on with the list."

"No. I really was running only on adrenaline for a while."

He got slowly and carefully to his feet. "I hope you didn't save what I was wearing. It was in pretty bad shape by that point, and it wasn't mine to begin with, either."

"No, we did scrap those rags. But we do have some clothes that should fit you perfectly, from our own captain."

Dylan froze. "Let me guess. He's not in this dimension, but in my dimension on my ship."

"So it seems."

He stared at her. "You're being awfully calm about this!"

"Sir, we already had our nice, healthy bout of hysteria and got it out of our systems."

That forced a laugh out of him. "If you don't mind, Dr. Travis, I'd like to get dressed now."

"Of course. Starin here," she gestured at a slim young man in an intern's uniform who gave him a tentative salute, "will happily escort you to the Command Deck when you think that you're ready."

Well. So far this was light-years ahead of the last dimension, and not as cloyingly pretty as the pacifist dimension.

Dylan shook his head, thinking back. What a long and convoluted journey this had been so far. He might have helped the saurians start on the road to peace. He'd violently opened the pacifists' eyes to reality. And he'd actually helped the last stand of humanity, the Nietzscheans, in the insectoid dimension.

I wish someone would help me *just about now!*

"Uh, sir . . . ?"

The youngster was eyeing him warily.

"I'm all right," Dylan said. "Tell you what, let's go see the Command Deck and get it over with."

"Uh, yes, sir."

The Command Deck looked almost alarmingly familiar. In fact, it looked almost exactly like his own Command Deck, at least if all the rough edges had been smoothed away and a fresh coat of paint had been applied to everything. And the crew . . .

Dylan staggered at the sight of them and had to brace himself against the doorframe. That was Beka, his Beka, her blonde hair gleaming gold, but with all the tension gone from her face and eyes. That was Trance, but a very serene and golden-skinned Trance. And Tyr . . . was that really Tyr, that tranquil-faced, dark-skinned man?

"I think I need to sit down," Dylan said.

"Of course," the alternate Beka said with a smile. "The command chair's yours, Captain Hunt."

He sat without ceremony. Damn, even the chair felt right. "I really think I need to know some more about this dimension, if you please."

Her smile brightened. "I can well understand that! First of all, Captain Hunt, our captain's name is Dylain Hunt. Yes, I know, that's pretty close. It startled us, too, believe me."

"I only hope my crew is treating him as well," Dylan said courteously.

"Oh, I'm sure that they are. Though I don't know what your dimension is like," she added, not quite prodding.

Dylan hesitated, wondering how honest he could be, wondering how much he could trust these people.

Oh hell, I give up, he decided suddenly. *Either they're honest or they're not. I'm tired of the whole mess.*

"Well, to begin," he said, "my ship is the *Andromeda Ascendant*."

"Ours is the *Andromeda Rising*," this dimension's Tyr commented.

"That is close!" Dylan agreed.

"It is, indeed," said a familiar voice.

"Rommie?"

It did look like her, but a slightly older Rommie in a simple, stylish pantsuit, her hair swept up in an elegant fashion.

"I am Romma," she said.

"Happy to meet you, Romma."

"Please, continue with your story. I would like to hear more about my sister ship."

"Of course. Now, she and I started out together on our voyage about three hundred years ago . . ."

When Dylan had finished his story, there was absolute silence on the Command Deck. Dylan looked about warily. "What? What's wrong?"

"Ah, nothing, Captain Hunt," the alternate Beka said. "It's just . . ."

"What? Go on, tell me," he added wryly, "I promise that you won't hurt my feelings."

"Well, it's just . . . our dimension's history seems to be a little bit more, ah, more upbeat than yours."

"Oh?"

"There are some amazing similarities between the two. This ship and our captain actually did go through a similar time distortion experience, three hundred years' worth, in fact. But after that, the differences really start adding up."

"Please, go on," Dylan prodded gently.

"Well, in our dimension, the Nietzscheans did go to war against the Commonwealth, just as they did in your dimension—but here, they went to war prematurely, with not all the clans in full agreement. And so, since the Nietzscheans weren't fully united as a military force, they were ultimately defeated, without either side being permanently damaged."

"But, wait a minute," Dylan interrupted in confusion, turning to the alternate Tyr. "You, now. In my dimension, your analog is a Nietzschean. Aren't you . . . ?"

"A Nietzschean also? Yes, I am." He smiled faintly, and there was a peace in his eyes that the Tyr that Dylan knew had never shown. "When my people realized they couldn't win the war without taking massive losses—too massive to be practical—we were forced to admit two truths: that unaugmented humans could be just as honorable and just as fierce in battle as we. It was quite a revelation for us, believe me.

"But by now, three hundred years later, we have become the Commonwealth's staunch allies, and they have helped us hold off any attackers. It's proved to be an alliance that benefits both partners."

"The Commonwealth!" Dylan exclaimed.

"Oh yes," the alternate Beka said. "Let me assure you, sir, that the Commonwealth has been restored and is indeed operating very well. In fact, our latest triumph has been the utter surrender and total retreat of the Magog."

"You're joking—no," Dylan corrected himself, "I can see that you're not joking. And I bet that you have a full crew, too."

"Ah, yes, sir, we do."

My God. This dimension is sounding more and more like every one of my dreams, so much so that . . .

No. What am I thinking? This isn't my dimension. I can't stay here. Hey, I couldn't even if I wanted . . .

Do I want to stay?

"You don't have to do anything about anything right now, sir," the alternate Tyr said consolingly. "Not yet. We can't go anywhere until the anomaly zone reopens anyhow."

True enough.

"All right then," Dylan said, testing. "In the meantime, I think that I would like to tour this *Andromeda*."

"Oh, of course," the alternate Beka said cheerfully. "Feel free to go anywhere you like. Would you like a guide?"

"No. Thank you." Still testing, Dylan added, "I would like to go touring on my own."

She smiled. "I can understand that. If you prefer a little solitude, sir, by all means! I suspect that our two ships are pretty close parallels. And if you do need anything—"

"Don't worry. I'll ask."

This ship really was similar to his own in its layout, so much so that he could almost fool himself into thinking he was home. It was once again eerie to see a full crew in the corridors, although this time they were more, well, human, more normal, than the pacifist crew had been. And they were, above all, content.

God, this is amazing.

Whoa, he recognized that young man. "Ah, excuse me," Dylan called.

The familiar figure stopped and turned. "Sir?"

"Harper? It is you!"

"Hey, you're the alternate captain! Geez, look at you! I mean, the resemblance between the two of you, you and my own captain, is really amazing. And yep, I'm Seamus Harper, all right." He grinned at Dylan. "I was just on the way to my lab. Want to join me?"

"Your, ah, lab?"

"Yep, a real one. Used to work out of one of the machine shops, but when I came up with the Frengi Lensewarping Analysis, well, I got upgraded."

"Now you sound exactly like the Harper I know!"

"He still working out of a machine shop?"

"I'm afraid so. For now." Dylan stopped short, looking about the gleaming, fully equipped laboratory. "Nice!"

"Captain Hunt, you know, I just had a sudden thought. You've been wandering around dimensions for, well . . ."

"A hell of a long time?" Dylan supplied.

"Yeah. That sums it up, I'd guess. So, in all that time, did anyone sit down and try to figure out how to get you back? I mean, actually do analyses?"

"We never seemed to have the time," Dylan admitted. "There was always someone attacking either them or me."

"Okay, then!" The alternate Harper's eyes lit up with eagerness, making him look exactly like the Harper Dylan knew. "No one's attacking us now. So let's see what we can find out! I bet I can get you home!"

While Harper worked, Dylan thought. This wasn't a perfect place, but it was undeniably head and shoulders above his own. A healthy Commonwealth. Friendly Nietzscheans. And no Magog. God, but he was tempted to stay.

But if you do, the other Dylan can't get back. Your Andromeda is stuck with the wrong captain, and he is stuck there with the wrong dimension.

Time passed while Harper happily made his calculations and worked out his equations.

"Uh, Captain Hunt?" he said suddenly.

It was the first time that Dylan had seen the young man look so somber. "Harper? What is it? What went wrong?"

"Oh, nothing. In fact, I just worked out the last of the calculations. Double-checked them, too, and they all add up properly, so you don't have to ask about that. But, well, it looks like you have a choice, Captain Hunt, and, uh, I don't think that it's going to be an easy choice for you to make, sir."

"Go on, Harper."

"Well. You can actually stay here."

"Oh, I knew that. It would mean that your captain would be stuck in my dimension, though. I couldn't do that to someone who's pretty much myself, my other self."

"No, sir, that's not exactly it." Harper licked his lips nervously. "What I mean is, you really can stay here. Like, forever. This will become your right dimension. The physics, the metaphysics, of the anomaly zone will allow that."

"But . . . ? Harper, please."

"But the reverberations of your choice will most likely kill the, ah, the other Captain Hunt, and take out that Andromeda as well. This will become the correct dimension, all right. And the only one."

For a long time, Dylan couldn't say a thing. To stay here, to fit neatly into a happier, more orderly universe . . .

To kill the people he knew, to destroy the ship that was his command . . .

To eliminate an entire dimension . . . ?

I can't do it.

"Never mind, Harper," Dylan said. "Let's just work out the calculations to get me home again."

And never mind that I feel as if I'm turning my back on paradise.

What the hell, he added silently, it wouldn't be the first time that a man was cast out of Eden.

TWENTY-ONE • THERE'S NO PLACE LIKE HOME

As far as we can discern, the sole purpose of human existence is to kindle a light in the darkness of mere being.

—CARL JUNG

He . . . was back on a Command Deck. It looked right in all details, but by now Dylan was no longer sure how he was going to know it really was the right deck, the right ship, the right dimension—

"Dylan!" a woman exclaimed fiercely. "Where the *hell* have you been?"

"Beka!" he said in immense relief. "Good to see you again, too."

I'm back, Dylan thought.

Greetings came pouring in from all over the ship:

"Captain Hunt! I prayed for your return!"

"Thank you, Bem."

"Yo, Captain, glad you got back."

"And it was an alternate you who got me here," Dylan told him.

"Hey, way to go! Too bad I can't shake his hand."

"I knew you'd return," Trance said softly.

"I, ah, I believe it," Dylan said.

"Welcome back."

Dylan grinned. He knew who'd muttered that last, grudging, greeting. "Thank you, Tyr. You would not have believed what your alternate selves were like."

But he didn't explain.

Just then, Rommie appeared in her usual exotic garb, and the biggest smile Dylan had ever seen on her AI's face. "Dylan! I'm delighted to see you. I was getting really tired of having alternate Dylans trying to paint me or hide in me or just be what I think you call a pain in the—"

"It's good to see you again, too, Rommie."

I'm really back in the right dimension. I'm really home.

And damn it, I am going to stay here!

"Beka," Dylan ordered, "get us out of here before that damned anomaly opens again."

She dropped into her seat. "You got it. I'm really tired of having to deal with all those alternate you's. You can be a real pain when you're not you," she added with a grin.

He sat back in the command chair, feeling utterly content, as *Andromeda*, his *Andromeda*, sped out of danger.

But suddenly Beka warned, "Ships on screen. Uh, Dylan, I

think that our mysterious enemies just found us again."

"They have," Rommie agreed.

Oh hell, Dylan thought. *I thought we were done with that.*

But then Dylan frowned, sitting forward, staring at the viewscreen. "Rommie, magnify that image if you would. A little more—yes. Hold that." He leaned forward even farther, studying it. Something about the script on the side of that ship looked awfully familiar. . . .

Yes, it was!

"I know those guys," he said. "They're this dimension's version of an insectoid race."

"Oh Lord," Beka muttered. "Not them again. We got one of them as an alternate you, and the damned bug tried to kill me. I didn't know they were in our dimension, too."

"Apparently a version of them is," Dylan said. "And I'd say that you probably know by now that they look on all humans as vermin."

Beka gave him a fierce, teeth-bared grin. "What say, Dylan? We're better armed than they are. Shall we blast them out of space?"

"No," Dylan said thoughtfully. "I don't think we need to waste the energy." He smiled ever so faintly. "I do believe I know how to get rid of them. Get me an open communications link, if you would."

"It's open."

"They can hear me?"

"They can hear you."

"Good. Hello, folks," Dylan broadcast. "This is the human

vermin hive-ship speaking. You know, I've figured you people out. You're afraid of us."

"Not," a flat voice retorted.

"Oh, you are. And you know something? You really should be. *We know your weaknesses.* Think of this, guys: Single-mind. All of you turned single-mind by us. No more group-mind, no more hive-ship. Each and every one of you torn from the others and left single-mind and alone. Forever alone, guys, each and every one of you. That's what we can do to you. Single-mind forever."

"Not!"

"Think we can't do it? Want to try us? Each of you want to be lost to the hive? Think about it. Single-mind forever."

"They're . . . retreating!" Rommie announced, sounding truly amazed. "No, they're doing more than that. They are fleeing!"

Dylan sat back again, laughing. "Oh, I just bet that they are. I just called their bluff, you see, and they bought it. And now they're sure that humans are too tough for them."

"Captain Dylan Hunt certainly is," Beka muttered.

"Why, Beka!"

"What? I didn't say anything."

But she was grinning.

Much, much later, after he'd told everyone his whole, convoluted series of stories and heard all of their stories in return, Dylan escaped alone to the Observation Deck. There, he stood silently for a long while, looking out into the splendor of space. Far ahead, a backlit nebula blazed with glorious reds and blues, and all around them, the blackness was spangled with stars.

Beautiful. Truly beautiful. We don't get much of a chance to just look out the window.

"Didn't know there was anyone else here," a gruff voice said suddenly.

"Tyr."

For a while, the two men stood together side by side in a rare moment of peace, looking out at the glory around them.

Then Tyr glanced sideways at Dylan and said, "Tell me this. Weren't you tempted?"

"Eh?"

"To stay in the ideal dimension, the 'right' one."

"Sure I was. But I didn't give in. This," Dylan said with great sincerity, "is the right dimension."

ABOUT THE AUTHOR

Josepha Sherman has written over thirty novels, featuring *Star Trek*, *Highlander*, *Buffy*, and *Xena* tie-ins. Her original titles include *Son of Darkness* and *The Shattered Oath*. She also has short story and anthology credits to her name, along with folklore, children's, and young adult novels. She currently lives in New York City.